Is Winona Ryder Still with the Dude from Soul Asylum?

and Other LURID Tales of TERROR and DOOM!!!

by Douglas Hackle

Other Books by Douglas Hackle

Clown Tear Junkies

The Hottest Gay Man Ever Killed in a Shark Attack

Is Winona Ryder Still with the Dude from Soul Asylum? and Other LURID Tales of TERROR and DOOM!!!

Copyright © 2017 by Douglas Hackle

All Rights Reserved. No part of this book may be reproduced or utilized in any form or by any means, electronic or mechanical, including photocopying, recording, or by any information storage and retrieval system, without permission in writing from the publisher. The exception would be the case of brief quotations embodied in critical articles or reviews and pages where permission is specifically granted by the publisher author. This is a work of fiction. Names, characters, businesses, places, events and incidents are either the products of the author's imagination or used in a fictitious manner. Any resemblance to actual persons, living or dead, or actual events is purely coincidental.

"The Powell/Fourth Dog Incident" originally appeared in *The Strange Edge Magazine Issue 0*.

"TERROR SARDINES in TERROR SAUCE," "The Many Bad Habits of My Main Man, Klin-Klat, A.K.A. the Tap Dance Kid," and "The Bored Ouija Bored" originally appeared in *The Bizarro Starter Kit – Red*.

"Not That It Matters, but the War of 1812 Was Kinda Hawt" originally appeared at *Kafka Review*.

"I Won the MegaSuperLotto" originally appeared at *The Strange Edge*.

"Got Me a Date with an Uptown Girl" originally appeared at *three minute plastic*.

"The Case of the Already-Solved Case" originally appeared at *Bizarro Central*.

TABLE OF CONTENTS

My Name Is Douglas 1

The Two Times I Was a Mean Man 3

Tokens 31

The Powell/Fourth Dog Incident 36

The Ghost, the Boulder, and the Glaive 55

TERROR SARDINES in TERROR SAUCE 63

Not That It Matters, but the War of 1812 Was Kinda Hawt 75

The Unpursued Person 87

I Won the MegaSuperLotto 99

A Small Owl with a Broken Wing (from Compton) 103

Is Winona Ryder Still with the Dude from Soul Asylum? 111

The Many Bad Habits of My Main Man, Klin-Klat, A.K.A. the Tap Dance Kid 122

This Puppet Puts the "P" in "Puppet" 125

Got Me a Date with an Uptown Girl 144

The Case of the Already-Solved Case 151

Flawless Face® 159

The Bored Ouija Board 165

TERROR THING 174

All Superhero Movies and Shows Are Fucking Boring, Zombies Are Lame, Cthulhu Is Stupid, and Everything Is Fucked 190

Our Hearts Will Go On, Yo 209

My Name Is Douglas

Yo, I got somethin' to say. And it goes a little bit like this:
UNO…DOS…TRES…QUAT—

My name is Douglas,
Pronounced with an uglas.
I'm on tha mic,
And I just don't give a fuglas.

Imma eat maggots,
While ur basic ass eats hummus.
Gonna stuff my mouth with crickets,
While u be whack and u be bugless.

And just like DAT BOI,
Imma roll up on a dank uni,
Doing sick on-fleek tricks,
Makin' u look dumb and whack and puny.

So don't be jelly
When I roll on through,
Nabbin' more ass than a goddamn zoo.

While you be stickin' worms on hooks
To catch some whack-ass fish,

I be eatin' worms and maggots
As tha main damn dish—*swish!*

And just like my dude
Edgar Allan fuckin' Poe,
Imma wash that shit down
With a cask of Amontillado, yo.

Yeah, I'm on tha mic,
Yup, I'm on tha conga,
And just like Nietzsche,
That which does not kill me makes me stronga.

Yo, I be havin' sex
while you be wankin' to computer-virus porn,
And just like motherfuckin' Yeats,
Imma slouch toward Bethlehem to be born.

To tha D,
To tha O,
To tha U,
To tha G.
Poppets is hustlaz,
And puppets is Gs.

Yeah, that's right, duuude,
I'm tha original Hacksta.
So best up ur game, G,
And take some lessons from tha masta.

The Two Times I Was a Mean Man

Not to boast, but I've always been a pretty nice guy. While most children don't develop empathy until six or seven years of age, I was troubled by the distresses of my older siblings as early as age two, or so my mother used to tell me. And at a time when my childhood peers were being taught through punishment and reward to repress their natural proclivity towards selfishness and cruelty, I was innately kind, generous, patient, tolerant, respectful, and courteous. Though not usually a target of bullies myself in grade school and high school, owing to my thick frame, my instinct was always to defend other kids from them, a practice that earned me more than a few black eyes and busted lips.

To this day, I still put the needs of others above my own. Do unto others as they would do unto you—and then some!—I say. Towards that end, I volunteer regularly for any charitable program or institution around town that will have me: homeless shelters, soup kitchens, no-kill animal shelters, retirement homes, group homes for special needs adults, you name it. I also perform volunteer work at the local library, tutor children at inner-city elementary schools, coach several underfunded youth sports teams, and help organize the annual Race for the Cure and Relay for Life events in my city. I even started my own local Meals on Wheels program a few years back.

Some might argue that I'm nice to a fault. Sure, I can see how my habit of hanging out on street corners just to wait for old ladies who'll need help crossing the street might be considered a tad excessive. By hey, what can I say? That sort of thing is my jam.

When dining out, I make it a point to tip unfriendly, inattentive servers at least twenty percent. Why? Because I haven't the dimmest clue what manner of life challenges such a waitress or waiter may be enduring outside of work or may soon be forced to endure.

I mean, who am I to judge, ya know?

I also make it a point to plant a tree every year on Arbor Day. (Just seems like a good thing to do, ya know?)

Now, I'm not saying I'm perfect. I've never claimed to be some sort of exemplar of selflessness, charity, and good behavior. However—and again, not to boast—I do have a pretty good track record as far as being a "do unto others" type of guy goes. In fact, I can only recall two times in my life when I was a mean man.

THE END

What?
You're still here?
You're still reading?
Ah, I see. You want to know more about the two times I was a mean man, huh? Well, sure ya do. I mean, I get it. I'm not stupid. Getting the dirt on someone is far more interesting than hearing about them planting trees or helping little old ladies across the street.

Alright. Though we are strangers separated by time and space, I somehow sense you're a good egg.

I'll tell you about the two times I was a mean man.

Here goes.

Act of Meanness #1 – The Cut Off

The first time in my life I was a mean man, I was driving home after working a long shift at the local Holla Dolla, a franchised dollar store chain. It had been a rough day. I was irritable, tired, hungry, and a little depressed. I just wanted to get home. Driving eastbound in the right lane of Salieri-*Krull* Boulevard (a four-lane road), I zoned out for a spell, stuck to the right when I should have changed lanes since I had to make a left at the approaching intersection.

When I snapped out of my fatigue-induced road trance, I realized I was about to overshoot the intersection. I was doing about fifty miles per hour, the light was green, and the westbound lanes were free of any oncoming traffic. I still had enough time to get over and make the turn, though the maneuver would require me to brake somewhat abruptly. Still, no big deal so long as no one was blocking me in the left lane.

I glanced at the left lane through my side mirror and saw a black '67 Cadillac cruising maybe two car lengths behind me.

Dang it, I thought. And then, for just a moment, I gave up on the idea of attempting to make the turn. Instead, I resigned myself to the inevitability of having to overshoot the intersection.

I'll just pull into the shopping plaza up ahead and turn around, I thought.

Now, that's what I *should've* done. That's what I normally *would've* done. And that's what I always *had* done in similar situations in the past.

But that's not what I did.

Just in the nick of time, I cut the steering wheel to the left while slamming on the brake pedal. The tires of my Honda Disaccord screeched as it careened from Salieri-*Krull* onto intersecting Dapperchild Avenue. This screech was echoed by the tires of the Caddy I'd just cut off while the driver of that big ol' beast of a car broke hard, veered sharply left, and drove up onto the median to avoid rear-ending me. If that wasn't bad enough, just as I came out of my wild turn, I held up a reverse middle finger for the driver to feast his or her eyes upon.

"Fuck you," I said dismissively, adding, "Don't like my fucking driving? Well, then go choke to death on big, sweet, blue dick, you motherfucker!"

That's what I actually said! Not only was this the first time I'd ever spoken harshly to or about another person, it was the first time I'd ever said a cuss! To this day, I still don't know what came over me that night. Had it been all those years of always helping others and being kind and patient and understanding? Had some darker, pent-up, heretofore unknown part of my psyche been seeking this release for some time now? Was the incident just the result of the cumulative effects of the normal stresses of everyday life finally catching up to me? I couldn't say then, and I still can't say now.

As I sped off, I glanced in the rearview mirror. Seeing that old car back at the intersection where it had been forced to stop, resting half on the median like some beached mechanical whale, those unprovoked and alien feelings of hostility and selfishness vanished from within me, feelings that had possessed me like some demonic presence. Shock, guilt, humiliation, and deep regret set in immediately to replace these exorcised negative emotions.

As if by delayed reaction, the driver of the Cadillac finally laid on the vehicle's bright hi-low horn:

BEEEEEEEEEEEEEEEEEEEEEEEEEEEEEEEEEEEEEEEEE....

Notice how there's no "P" in the above "*BEEP.*" That's because even as the Caddy turned and barreled down Dapperchild Avenue after me, even as it tailgated me all the way back to my house that night, even as the car—still riding my ass like a diaper—followed me into my driveway, even then the driver did not let up on that horn.

EEEEEEEEEEEEEEEEEEEEEEEEEEEEEEEEEE....

I put my car into park and sat still for a moment, staring into the rearview mirror and listening to that blaring horn, the illumination provided by the lamppost in my driveway allowing me to see the deep black tint of the Caddy's windshield for the first time. Part of me was scared, picturing some brawny tough ass sitting behind the tinted glass, snorting like a bull and getting ready to charge. If I got out of my car, would this road rager jump out and attack me? He might have a knife on him. A gun even. Part of me wanted to take this opportunity to apologize. And yet still another part of me was thinking: *Fuck this dude. Yeah, I totally cut him off and flipped him the bird. I was completely in the wrong. But that's no reason to go all road-rage psycho on someone. Get the fuck over it, pal, and get the fuck out of my driveway!*

I eventually climbed out of my car, shut the door, turned to face the Caddy. I tried shouting, "I'm sorry!" over the peal of the horn, held up my open palms, shrugged my shoulders, and cocked my head to the side as if to add, *Hey, it is what it is.* I stood there for a few beats, peering into the impenetrable black of that broad windshield, waiting for someone to get out of the car or for the damn thing to back out of my driveway or for that horn to finally cease its braying, waiting for something—anything—to happen.

But the horn just blared on.

EEEEEEEEEEEEEEEEEEEEEEEEEEEEEE
EEEEEEEEEEEE...

"Suit yourself," I said, shaking my head as I turned to go into my house.

***

I nuked a frozen burrito, grabbed a can of PBR from the fridge, and sat on my living room couch, where I drew the shades back so I could watch the Caddy while I ate. It was nearly midnight. About ten minutes later, Rich Perkins, my neighbor from across the street, came marching up my driveway in his pajamas and slippers. Obviously very pissed off, he halted at the side of the Caddy and knocked on the driver's window, which I noticed was as darkly tinted as the rest of the car's windows. I set my beer down on the coffee table, grabbed my katana from its wall mount above the fireplace, unsheathed it, and made for my front door.

"Are you crazy?" Rich screamed as he slammed the butt of his hand repeatedly on the driver's window. "Lay off that fucking horn already! You woke up my kids. You're gonna wake up this whole goddamn neighborhood!"

All ninja-like, I crouch-jogged up to Rich, gripping the katana's long handle tightly in both hands. Before the man even had a chance to turn his head and notice me, I raised the blade high above my head and brought it down. My intent was only to warn him not to mess with the Caddy driver—I certainly did not want to kill this innocent father of four. But sometimes a lesson learned hard is a lesson learned well. As such, I took my neighbor's nose off with one clean slash.

"Leave him the fuck alone, Rich!" I yelled at the man, who was too stunned to scream as he backpedaled from the Caddy, cupping the gaping triangle-shaped hole that was now in his face with both his hands, hot blood spilling down over his lips and chin.

I pointed at the Caddy. "I cut this car off earlier tonight, Rich. Ran it half off the fucking road. The driver has every right to be here laying on the horn like this. So pick up your goddamn nose, go home, and call yourself an ambulance. If the noise continues to be a problem, give your kids some fucking earplugs or something. Deal with it!"

"Okay, I...I will. Sorry, Mitch. I didn't know that you cut this car off earlier." Rich picked up his nose and ran home.

I turned to the Caddy's driver-side window. "Sorry about that," I said before heading back into my house.

EEEEEEEEEEEEEEEEEEEEEEEEEEEE...

Some other busybody on my street must have called the cops soon after that, because just as I lay down in bed twenty minutes later, two patrol cars rolled up in front of my house, their flashers bathing my bedroom ceiling in stroboscopic red and blue light. By the time I hopped out of bed, threw some clothes on, grabbed my Glock from the closet, and ran outside, the boys in blue already had their guns drawn while the driver of the Caddy still lay on that horn, refusing to open the door.

From my front stoop, I carefully raised my pistol, aimed, and fired a shot at one of the four policemen surrounding the Caddy. It was a warning shot aimed at the cop's crotch, certainly not intended to kill the man. Always a good marksman, my aim was true, the .45-cal hollow-point round from my Glock obliterating the cop's genitals in a sick explosion of flesh, skin, blood, and semen. Dude dropped his gun as he doubled over and fell screaming onto my lawn.

With my piece still pointed in their general direction, I yelled, "Hey, I cut this Cadillac off earlier with my car, ran it half off the road. The driver has every right to be here in my driveway laying on the horn like that. If anything, while you guys are here you should write *me* a ticket for my reckless driving earlier. But leave the fucking Caddy driver alone or else my next shot isn't going to be a warning shot. You hear me, you assholes!"

"We hear you," one of the cops said. Two of them went to help their fallen brother while the remaining officer wrote me up a ticket for reckless driving.

An ambulance arrived soon after to transport the—in all likelihood—permanently emasculated cop to the hospital, at which time the other cops vacated the scene too.

With that ticket in my hand, I felt much better about the whole incident, since I had just been punished for my uncharacteristic asshole behavior of earlier that night. I walked up to the Caddy driver's window, held the ticket up to the ebony glass. "See?" I yelled, waving it. "This should make you feel a little better. I'm down twenty-five hundred bucks! I'd say that's fair comeuppance for what I did to you."

Maybe now the driver would finally take his or her hand off that goddamn horn, back out of my driveway, and go the fuck home.

But as I lay in bed an hour later, still listening to the abrasive bawl of that horn (muted—thankfully—somewhat by the walls of my house), I realized that paying the local traffic court twenty-five hundred bucks would not necessarily do anything to mitigate the Caddy driver's anger, aggravation, and distress. Some folks hold grudges for a long, long time. And then there are those who are altogether incapable of forgiveness. Was the Caddy driver such a person?

Only time would tell.

EEEEEEEEEEEEEEEEEEEEEEEEEE....

***

I always loved waking up to the calming, somewhat unearthly wail of a train horn when a freight train happened to pass along the south edge of town, and that's exactly what I thought I heard the next morning when I woke with a stretch and a yawn. A few moments passed before I realized the sound was not a train.

I climbed out of bed and parted the curtains of my bedroom window, which looked out onto my front yard.

There was that black Caddy just where I'd left it the night before, horn still blaring.

Famished, I went downstairs to cook myself a breakfast of scrambled eggs, sausage links, hash browns, toast, and coffee. As I ate at my kitchen table and watched the news on a small TV, I realized the Caddy driver might be hungry too. *What the heck*, I thought as I got up to grab a plate and silverware from the dishwasher.

In my slippers, pajama bottoms, and t-shirt, I walked out to the Caddy carrying a steaming plate of breakfast food. I knocked on the driver's window.

"Hey, you hungry?" I yelled over the wail of the horn. I waited for nearly a minute, but the driver neither opened the door nor unrolled the dark window.

"I'll tell ya what," I shouted, "One knock means 'yes.' Two knocks mean 'no.' Three knocks means 'I don't know.'" I paused. "Do you want breakfast?"

Immediately, a single, hard knock sounded from the window.

"Okay. Well, I guess you'll have to roll down the window for me to give this to you. Can you do that?"

One knock again. I waited a spell, but the window did not roll down. It took me a moment to read between the lines.

"Ah, do you want me to look away so I don't see you?"

One knock.

I held the plate close to the window and craned my neck so I was looking up at my chimney. I listened to the squeaky sound of the driver's window manually unrolling to about the halfway point. The driver then took the plate from my hand and quickly cranked the window back up. Needless to say, I wanted so badly to take a peek while this was happening, but I resisted temptation, not wishing to betray any trust I might be developing between the two of us.

I walked back to my house. But before I reached my side door, I paused, turned around, and returned to the Caddy.

"Hey, do you want a cup of coffee with that?" I shouted at the driver's window.

One knock.

"You take cream?"

Two knocks.

"Sugar?"

One knock.

"How many spoonfuls?"

One knock.

"Alrighty then. A cup o' joe with cream and a spoonful of sugar comin' right up."

And that horn just kept on bellowing through it all: a constant reminder that, despite my generous hospitality, the admittance of my wrongdoing, and that expensive reckless driving ticket I got last night, I was still being punished.

After I took away the Caddy driver's empty plate and coffee mug about fifteen minutes later (again, at the driver's insistence, I turned away from the window so as not to see him or her) I yelled, "Hey, I can see you're not done honking your horn at me. That's fine. I understand. But I have to leave for work in a few minutes. Could you back up so I can get out of my driveway?"

One knock.

"Great, thanks."

The Caddy driver was true to his or her word (or knock, I should say). The car backed out of the driveway as soon as I got into mine. But once I was on the road, the Caddy was right back on my ass. As I expected, it followed me to work and parked next to me in the Holla Dolla parking lot, horn howling as if to wake the dead.

***

The only products found on the shelves of Holla Dolla were one dollar bills. Some were older, more wrinkled, and more torn up than others, but each was worth exactly one dollar. Yet the price stickers on these dollars indicated prices ranging from $1.01 to $700. In the last two weeks, business had been slow. I wasn't sure why, but I suspected that maybe people were getting smarter, finally realizing what a scam it was to sell a one dollar bill for anything other than a dollar. I had been wise to the swindle since I started working at the dollar store years ago and hated the whole crooked racket. I especially loathed my store manager, Mr. Cruthers, who had no qualms about taking advantage of stupid people, mentally disabled people, and non-English-speaking immigrants who just didn't know any better. But unfortunately, I'd been unable to find a new job due to the shit economy even though I searched for jobs whenever I wasn't working at the store or doing volunteer work.

Anyhow, by the time Mr. Cruthers arrived that morning at around 10:45 AM, I had only sold two dollar bills: one for $1.25 and another for $14.23. After parking his van in his reserved spot, he got out with an angry red face and set his arms akimbo, glowering at the Caddy. Though I couldn't hear him, I saw him yelling as he stomped over to the Caddy's door and knocked on the window. Needless to say, I was obligated to leave my post at the checkout counter and make for the front door.

"Lay off that fucking horn, asshole!" Mr. Cruthers hollered. "And get the hell out of my lot!"

I opened the door and poked my head outside. "Mr. Cruthers! Leave that Caddy alone. It's okay for the driver to hang on the horn like that. See, last night when I was driving home, I—"

"This is okay, you say?" Mr. Cruthers interrupted as he stopped knocking on the window momentarily to look my way. "Are you fucking crazy, Smith? This jerk-off's gonna scare away our customers. Mind your own business and get the fuck back to work. I'll handle this."

He left me with no choice. I slipped back inside, lifted that clunky, old-fashioned cash register off the checkout counter, and waddled back outside bearing the heavy contraption in my arms. Now, I didn't want to kill Mr. Cruthers (well, maybe I did want to kill him, but only in that hyperbolic, nonliteral sense that everyone wants to kill their boss), so when I brought the register down onto his unsuspecting head, I only used about half my strength. I just wanted to give the man a warning.

He collapsed next to the Caddy, half his head more or less obliterated, the cash register now embedded in what remained of his skull.

"Leave the Caddy driver the fuck alone!" I shouted down at Mr. Cruthers' convulsing, pants-pissing, bowel-evacuating body. Gesturing toward the Caddy, I said, "Last night I cut this car off, ran it half off the fucking road. So the driver has every right to be here laying on the horn like this."

After warning my boss to leave the Caddy driver alone, I called him an ambulance. I learned later that day that the embedded cash register actually saved Mr. Cruthers' life by preventing him from bleeding to death. The surgeons who examined him determined that removing the cash register from his half-head would have killed the man. Mr. Cruthers would just have to live out the rest of his life as a deaf, dumb, blind, cash register-headed imbecile.

Obviously, Mr. Cruthers could no longer manage the store, so the dollar store had to fire him and bring in a new manager. Mr. Cruthers now lives at a nearby assisted living care facility, one for which I sometimes do volunteer work. And in an ironic twist of fate, even though that sorry motherfucker no longer works at Holla Dolla, he subsequently became one of the store's most loyal customers.

The store received a new cash register after the old one essentially became Mr. Cruthers' new head. Its replacement was a brand new, fancy schmancy, computerized point-of-sale system, and I hated the damn thing. And although I didn't miss working under Mr. Cruthers, I did miss that clunky old cash register. So when Mr. Cruthers came stumbling, mumbling, and drooling into the store every other week to throw away his entire disability paycheck on a few greasy, crumpled-up dollar bills, I always made sure to ring him up on the cash register that was his new head, just for old times' sake.

***

Anyhow, the incidents with my neighbor, the police, and Mr. Cruthers were just the beginning. Everywhere I drove, that black Caddy followed, its trumpeting horn as constant as the spin of the Earth. When I went to see a movie at the local drive-in theater a month later, the Caddy was right there beside me. Unfortunately, to stop the angry theater manager from harassing the Caddy driver, I had to set the dude's face on fire. Of course, I immediately helped put out said fire as I only intended to warn the man, to get him to back the fuck off and chill. When my grandmother passed away three months after that, the priest who officiated over her graveside burial service gave us similar grief. Understandably, I suppose, this man of the cloth did not appreciate having to shout over the Caddy's booming horn. He accused the driver of having respect neither for the deceased nor for us mourners. Now, I didn't want to kill the priest, obviously, but I had to do something. Luckily, I'd thought ahead and brought along a pail of concentrated hydrofluoric acid for just such an emergency. I promptly dumped the acid over the priest's head, reprimanding him as he screamed, writhed, melted, and steamed on the ground, before calling him an ambulance.

What choice did I have but to adjust to my new life with the black Caddy and its steadfast horn? So adjust I did. And though whole years ticked by, I never once complained about the situation. Not to myself, not to other people, not to the gods, and certainly not to the Caddy driver. I had no one to blame but myself for this state of affairs. I—who had been in such a big fucking hurry to get home that fateful night—was the transgressor, the trespasser, the offender, the wrongdoer, the asshole. So even if that black Caddy and its accursed horn ended up following me to my grave, then so be it.

And that's probably what would have happened if I hadn't won the Puppetball jackpot seven years later.

Which brings me to the second time in my life I was a mean person.

Act of Meanness #2 – That Time I Went Off on Janet (a Gas Station Attendant) for No Good Reason

I rarely played the lottery, and I pitied the sorry-ass, stupid, poor-ass motherfuckers who wasted so much of their hard-earned cash on it each and every week. However, on occasion, I'd drop a few bucks on the Mega Millions, the Powerball, or the Puppetball when the jackpots grew really big. Seven summers after I cut off that Caddy, the Puppetball jackpot reached a record-breaking 1.6 billion! After taxes, the lump sum payout for the jackpot would be an astounding 983.5 million puppets! Needless to say, I had to spend at least a buck to get in on that.

I pulled into the Shell station near my house on my way home from doing volunteer work at a no-kill animal shelter one Saturday afternoon, the Caddy hot on my tail. The parking lot was crowded since the big Puppetball drawing was scheduled for 11:00 PM that night. After I found a parking space, I got out of my car and went over to the Caddy driver's window.

"Hey, I'm gonna play the Puppetball," I shouted over the horn. "Jackpot is up to 1.6 billion. Do you want me to get you a ticket?"

One knock.

"How many sets of numbers do you want?"

Forty knocks.

"Really? You sure you wanna drop forty bucks on it? The odds of winning are astronomically horrible. I was just going to spend a buck myself."

One knock.

"Suit yourself," I held my hand near the window and averted my eyes. This was how we always did things, and I still had yet to see the driver's face or hear his or her voice.

The window rolled down partway, and the driver placed some bills in my hand. I waited for the window to close before counting them: a twenty, a ten, and four singles.

"Hey, you're six bucks short."

No knocks, which I interpreted to mean: *FUCK YOU, ASSHOLE!*

"Alright, alright, I'll put it on your tab." Fucker already owed me over three grand, which I realized I'd probably never see. But such was my lot.

Inside the gas station, I waited in line with all the other assholes who were there to buy Puppetball tickets. They had two people working two registers that night. Janet, my favorite clerk at the station, was busy busting her butt back there to make sure the lines moved along at least semi-quickly.

Judging from the looks of her, Janet was in her late 40s to early 50s and had been around the block a few times. Her long, frizzy, auburn hair was streaked gray and perpetually tied back in a bushy ponytail. The woman's deeply lined face and somewhat leathery skin suggested she either was or had been a heavy drinker and/or heavy smoker. She'd worked at this particular Shell station ever since I'd been patronizing it, which had to be the better part of five years. I often saw Janet in the morning when I stopped in to get coffee and in the evening when I stopped for beer. We didn't know each other well, but Janet always greeted me with a smile, and we often exchanged pleasantries about the weather and whatnot. She was just a nice, hardworking, working-class American—the salt of the earth—and I had absolutely nothing against her.

So that's why I can't explain what happened when I stepped up to her register that evening.

"Hi, Mitch," Janet said. "Whatcha need?"

"Hi, Janet. Forty-one autopicks for the Puppetball, please."

She took the thin stack of bills from my hand, counted them as she deposited the money in her register. She rapidly tapped the touch screen on the lottery machine, causing it to spit out the lottery tickets.

"Here ya go," she said, handing me the tickets. "Good luck."

Now would have been the time for me to say, "Thanks. Have a good one, Janet," and then go on my miserable way. But instead I stood there holding the Puppetball tickets, staring at Janet as my pursed lips drew themselves into a long frown.

"You need something else, honey?" she asked.

I didn't say anything yet as that frown screwed itself into a quivering scowl, a wave of seething anger rising from deep within me.

"I b-b-bet you live in a tr-tr-tr-trailer park," I finally stuttered under my breath.

"Sorry, what was that?" Janet asked. She leaned in bit, turned an ear to me.

"I said I bet you live in a fuckin' trailer park," I said, raising my voice this time, though I spoke through clenched teeth.

The woman was taken aback for a beat. "So what if I do?" she asked.

"I bet you never even finished high school," I said.

She gaped at me, slack-jawed.

"I bet you have five different kids from five different fathers. I bet you were a fucking grandmother before you even turned forty."

"I was thirty-seven," she said without hesitation, not proudly per se, but without an iota of shame. It was obvious she was trying her best to stand up to me.

"I bet you're a drunk. And...and a methhead. I bet your kids cook meth."

She didn't have anything to say to that, her weary, bloodshot eyes starting to tear up.

Janet had two crappy tattoos—well, at least two crappy tattoos that were visible: a rose on the side of her neck and a butterfly on her freckled forearm. I pointed at them and said, "And those tattoos you have, they're fucking stupid. They're fucking retarded!" My voice shook from the completely irrational, entirely unprovoked rage that continued to mount inside me. "Your whole existence is fucking stupid, Janet! You're just an ignorant, alcoholic, old, slutty bag of bitch-bones! You're nothing but a white trash, methwhore, fuck-witch!

WHY DON'T YOU JUST FUCKING KILL YOURSELF ALREADY, JANET?"

So saying, I spun around and stomped away, leaving that poor woman speechless behind the counter. All eyes in the store were on me as I made my way to the door. A family of five—a father, mother, and their three young children—happened to come into the gas station just as I was about to walk out.

Though I didn't know these people, I paused to lay my hands on the shoulders of one of the kids—a boy of about six years of age—and drew him close to me before addressing his parents. "I need to borrow your son."

"For how long?" the father asked.

"I'm not sure."

"As long as it's not for more than seven years," the father said.

"Shouldn't be that long. I'll try to get him back to you in five years."

"Here's my cell phone number," the father said, handing me his business card. "Just call me when you're done with him."

Taking the boy by the hand, I dragged him out of the gas station. By the time I got the kid buckled up in the backseat of my Honda Disaccord, I was already beginning to feel a terrible sting of guilt due to my uncalled-for, completely inexcusable mistreatment of Janet.

And during that whole time, the black Caddy was all EEEEEEEEEEEEEEEEEEEEEEE....

***

So there you have it: the two times in my life when I was a mean man. Not too shabby of a record though, huh? Nevertheless, as the years continue to roll by, effectively dulling all my memories, I don't ever want to forget about those two shameful low points. Perhaps that's why I've recorded them here in this manuscript: so that I'll always have a written record to remind me of those two shameful missteps of my past, thereby lessening the chance that I'll ever be a mean man again in the future. For many years, the omnipresence of that horning-blasting Caddy fulfilled that function well enough. But, alas, the Caddy's driver is no more.

THE END

What?
You're still there?
You're still reading, huh?
Oh, I see. You wanna know what happened to the Caddy driver?
Alright. Even though we are strangers separated by time and space, I can sense you're a real standup dude/dudette.
I'll tell you what happened to the Caddy driver.
Here goes.

***

When I arrived home that night after insulting Janet at the gas station, I promptly dressed up the borrowed boy like a clown. See, the reason I'd borrowed the kid in the first place was because I needed a houseclown, which is basically a kid clown who hangs around your house looking creepy while helping out with the household chores and not speaking unless spoken to. After I transformed the boy into a diminutive clown—face paint, rainbow afro wig, big red nose, floppy shoes, the whole nine yards—we sat down together on my living room couch to watch the live Puppetball drawing.

I nearly had a heart attack as I looked down at my ticket and heard all eight of my numbers announced on the TV.

I won!

I won the Puppetball!

Giddy with joy, I immediately ran outside to tell the Caddy driver the good news.

And as it turned out, I had the only winning ticket, so I didn't have to split the jackpot with anyone. I elected to receive the lump sum payout, which, as I mentioned before, was an incredible 983.5 million puppets!

A few days after I claimed my prize, the puppets arrived in a caravan of dump trucks and semis. Scores of deliverymen spent hours unloading the things. They filled my entire three-story 3,000-square-foot house from basement to attic with puppets so that I couldn't even go inside it anymore. They stuffed my attached garage and tool shed from floor to ceiling with puppets. They dumped and scattered puppets all over my land, transforming my ten flat acres into a rolling puppetscape comprised of dunes and valleys formed from every sort of puppet imaginable: marionettes, ventriloquist dummies, finger puppets, hand puppets, arm puppets, sock puppets, rod puppets, black light puppets, carnival puppets, shadow puppets, Punches, Judies, Japanese bunraku puppets, Indonesian Motekar puppets, Indian Rajasthani puppets, and more! Not only those, but the lottery commission embraced a rather broad definition of the word "puppet," so that the jackpot also included other puppet-like things, among them dolls (toy, antique, voodoo, sex, et al), mannequins, effigies, and an untold variety of figurines.

For three days, my houseclown and I had a grand ol' time puppeteering our own puppet shows, climbing puppet-dunes and rolling back down again, and playing hide-and-go-seek in the labyrinth of puppet-valleys that was now my yard. For my part, I also made sweet love to dozens of sex dolls, among them a really large blow up doll modeled after a morbidly obese Asian man.

The jackpot included *every* type of puppet that existed on the planet, including TERROR PUPPETS from TERROR TOWN. These infamous, unholy, terrifying abominations of nature did not emerge until three days after all the puppets were delivered, climbing free from the puppet-dunes like little zombies from their graves. I'd attempt to describe here what TERROR PUPPETS looked like, but my limited powers of description could not do them justice. Suffice it to say that TERROR PUPPETS lived up to their name.

After freeing themselves from the puppet-dunes, these ferocious, demonic, little killing machines found my houseclown first, swarmed him like a school of starving piranha. Poor kid! There was nothing I could do to help him. I hid at the top of a puppet-dune, peeking over the top as I watched the screaming boy get skeletonized in the space of a minute.

Drawn to the sound of the horn, the TERROR PUPPETS went after the Caddy driver next. The car was in my driveway, invisible beneath a heavy drift of puppets. But that didn't stop the TERROR PUPPETS. They rapidly exhumed the Caddy in a puppet-flinging frenzy. Once the car was unburied, the diabolical imps broke through the windshield and dragged the driver out onto the hood.

I couldn't believe my eyes. Though I had not so much as thought about the dude in decades, it turned out I actually knew the Caddy driver: I had gone to grade school and high school with him!

His name was Sissyboy Fussypants Jr. In fact, Sissyboy Fussypants Jr. had been one of my many...

...*victims*?

It all started coming back to me in a flood of long-repressed memories.

Seems I wasn't such a good person after all.

Remember when I said I developed empathy at a very young age? Well, I *still* hadn't developed empathy. Not an ounce. And all that volunteer work I claimed to do? That was bullshit too: I'd never done a charitable act in my entire life. Helping little old ladies cross the street and coming to the defense of bullied kids? Um, yeah, I'm afraid not. Indeed, I now recalled that although I'd approached little old ladies at crosswalks on numerous occasions, I'd done so only to beat them down to a red pulp with a goddamn stick! I also now recalled that all throughout my school years I'd been a bully of the most sadistic, cruelest sort imaginable.

Remember when I said I did volunteer work at a no-kill animal shelter on the same day I insulted Janet at the gas station? Indeed, I had visited a no-kill animal shelter that day.

But only *to kill all the goddamn animals!*

Rotten to the core since the day I was born, I was a goddamn, bona fide psychopath!

How many sorry-ass motherfuckers had been forced to eat dogshit and bloodied tampons at my latex gloved hands? This business about me being a mean man only two times in my life? Pfft. Completely false. Planting a tree every year on Arbor Day? Ha! On the contrary, I now recollected that I'd made it a point *to start a fucking forest fire* every year on Arbor Day. But evidently I'd manufactured this false goody two shoes version of myself at some point in my past, maybe as a defense mechanism against the guilt I eventually began to feel about being such a horrible, rotten son of a bitch.

Well, I sure as hell wasn't guilty about anything anymore.

As I gaped at Sissyboy Fussypants Jr. sprawled out on the hood of the Caddy, I remembered with increasing clarity and detail how I used to make this guy's life a living hell. No wonder the dude had been so persistent in following me around and laying on his horn like that all these years. Sissyboy Fussypants Jr.! That was his real name! Yes, the name his batshit-insane parents actually gave him at birth! And as you might guess, the dude's egghead dad was named Sissyboy Fussypants Sr. I mean, how could you *not* bully someone named Sissyboy Fussypants Jr.? How could you not want to bash someone named Sissyboy Fussypants Jr. into a red fucking paste on the goddamn sidewalk?

But it wasn't just the dude's goofy name or the fact that he was a weak and defenseless dork that bugged the shit out of me. See, Sissyboy was also a complete freak and should have never been allowed to attend school with normal kids.

Perhaps some explanation is in order. Severely deformed at birth, Sissyboy had a hospice where his left arm should have been. And I'm not talking about a small, human arm-sized hospice. I'm talking about a 40,000-square-foot, fully functioning, fully staffed, very real hospice with very real people dying inside of it.

Where the dude's right arm should have been was the War of 1812 riding a skateboard. Yes, the actual War of 1812 riding an actual skateboard. I know that doesn't make a lick of fucking sense. But like I said, this dude was a freak of epic proportions.

In place of Sissyboy's left leg was the 2,327th time George Washington cranked one off in his colonial outhouse when it was like fucking twenty below zero with the wind chill while Martha Washington waited in the house for him thinking he'd just gone out to take a dump. And I don't mean that in place of a left leg Sissyboy had some sort of holographic recording of the 2,327th time George Washington cranked one off in his colonial outhouse when it was like fucking twenty below zero with the wind chill while Martha Washington waited in the house for him thinking he'd just gone out to take a dump. Rather, in place of Sissyboy's left leg was the *actual occurrence* of George Washington beating his meat for the 2,327th time in his colonial outhouse when it was like fucking twenty below zero with the wind chill while Martha Washington waited in the house for him thinking he'd just gone out to take a dump.

Remember when Alanis Morissette was publicly executed in Canada (boiled alive in a giant vat of maple syrup, to be exact) for ironically misusing the word "ironic" in her hit single "Ironic"? Well, where Sissyboy's right leg should have been was that public execution. Again, I'm not talking about some sort of holographic representation here. I'm talking about the actual occurrence of said public execution of Alanis Morissette.

The sorry motherfucker's body was the Mississippi River (yes, the ENTIRE FLIPPIN' MISSISSIPPI RIVER— from Minnesota to the Gulf of Mexico!), while his head was a Chicken McNugget that had been dipped in white dogshit, set on fire, and flung off the top of the Eiffel Tower.

I mean, could anyone have resisted bullying a freak of this magnitude? I don't think so. And as I watched the TERROR PUPPETS begin to beat his sorry ass to a red paste, I couldn't help but feel that old bloodlust again.

I stood up on the apex of the puppet-dune I'd been hiding behind, cupped my hands around my mouth, and called out, "Hey, wait for me! I wanna help too!" With that, I tumbled headlong down the steep face of the dune and scrambled to my feet at its base.

Together, the TERROR PUPPETS and I beat Sissyboy's ass to a red paste. And although we didn't kill the severely deformed man, we mortally wounded him.

Sissyboy didn't have long to live, maybe a few days at the most, so it was very convenient that in place of the man's left arm was a fully functioning hospice. When we finished beating him to a red paste, we simply (if impossibly) admitted him to the hospice, where the experienced and wonderful staff there made him feel quite comfortable, all things considered.

We visited Sissyboy, paid our last respects to him shortly after the nurses got him settled in his room. After we exited that gray, depressing building, we enjoyed a dinner of maple syrup-boiled Alanis Morissette atop a puppet-dune that afforded a scenic view of the city.

That night, like so many mischievous children at a sleepover, the TERROR PUPPETS wanted to stay up late. But I insisted we all get to bed early. See, the following day was Arbor Day, and I wanted my new little toy soldiers and me to be well-rested for the fun-filled day I had planned for us, a day that would consist of force-feeding dogshit and bloodied tampons to any sorry-ass motherfuckers unlucky enough to cross our path, beating people down to red fucking smears on sidewalks, setting fucking forest fires, saying unkind things to people, and just generally being as mean as we could possibly be.

Tokens

Once upon a time, there was an extremely well-developed character, a token black guy, and token gay guy.

The extremely well-developed character was so well developed, in fact, that he was *perfectly* developed. He was the only perfectly developed character in the history of literature. Psychologically intricate, emotionally complex, morally conflicted, unpredictable, and unforgettable in all the right ways, he was the complete opposite of a stock character. He jumped off the page, as they say.

Jay Gatsby, Stephen Dedalus, Captain Ahab, Humbert Humbert, Atticus Finch—those guys didn't have shit on this dude.

In sharp contrast to him, the token black guy and the token gay guy were underdeveloped, two-dimensional, insultingly stereotypical, and forgettable to the point of being nonentities. So it should come as no surprise that the token black guy and the token gay guy eventually became jealous of the perfectly developed character.

"Let's go fuck that sucka's shit up, my main man," the token black guy said to the token gay guy.

"If you thay tho, token black guy," the token gay guy lisped. "Leth go fuck that thucka'th shit up."

So the token black guy and the token gay accosted the perfectly developed character and beat the living crap out of him. They beat his perfectly rendered ass down to a pulpy pile of perfectly rendered blood, guts, bone, sinew, fat, skin, hair, shit, chyme, chyle, piss, semen, and tears.

Soon after they beat the perfectly developed character to death, the two token characters grew bored. They wanted to do something fun, but they had not a cent between them.

"Man, we be broke," the token black guy said. "What da fuck we gonna do now, muthafucka?"

"Hey, I got an idea," the token gay guy said. "We may not have any money, but we're both made out of Chuck E. Cheeth tokenth. Leth go to Chuck E. Cheeth and play thome gameth!"

What he said was true. Both the token black guy and the token gay guy were made out of Chuck E. Cheese tokens.

That's why they were called the token black guy and the token gay guy.

So they went to Chuck E. Cheese forthwith, where they pried tokens from each other's heads, torsos, and limbs to play the games.

As the afternoon wore on, their once fully formed anthropomorphic shapes became more and more like stick figures as they deposited more of themselves into the machines. After playing skee ball and *Basketball Frenzy* for about an hour, they stuck to classic arcade games like *Frogger*, *Donkey Kong*, *Pac-Man*, *Ms. Pac-Man*, *Pac-Non-Gendered Person*, *Tron*, *Mortal Kombat II*, *Mortal Kombat IV*, *Street Fighter II*, *Escape from the Assisted Living Center*, *Escape from the Nursing Home*, *Escape from the Hospice*, *Escape from the Hospice II*, *Escape from the Funeral Parlor*, *Escape from the Crematorium*, *Escape from the Crematorium III*, and *Escape from the Grave VII*.

They won a shit-ton of tickets playing those games. In fact, between the two of them, the token black guy and the token gay guy collected a million tickets that day, which was enough to snag the most valuable prize available: a live, fully grown adult polar bear that had naturally purple fur, a giant stapler for a head, naturally swastika-shaped eyes on its giant stapler head, and a vicious, snapping, super-charged electric eel for a tail.

After the token gay guy redeemed their million tickets at the merchandise counter, a miserable, zit-faced Chuck E. Cheese wage slave freed the polar bear from its cage back in the storeroom, allowing the monster to stampede out into the crowded restaurant.

That stapler-headed, electric eel-tailed, purple polar bear proceeded to slaughter all the babies, children, and adults in the restaurant, including the staff, either by stapling their faces with staples the size of toasters or electrocuting them with that super-charged electric eel tail. After it killed everyone but the token black guy and the token gay guy, the bear used its terrible but cute claws to rend its victims' bodies to bits and pieces.

But this all worked out rather well for the token black guy and the token gay guy, as they were getting sick of waiting in the long lines that had formed in front of some of the more popular games, games like *Frogger*, *Donkey Kong*, and *After You Kill Me and Bury Me in the Woods, Please Don't Dig Up My Body a Year Later and Poke It with a Stick!* Now they didn't have to wait to play anything!

Soon after everyone was dead, all that remained of the token black guy and the token gay guy were two floating pairs of hands made out of Chuck E. Cheese tokens. Eventually and inevitably, the token black guy and the token gay guy were each reduced to a single Chuck E. Cheese token. When that occurred, they deposited themselves into *After You Kill Me and Bury Me in the Woods, Please Don't Dig Up My Body a Year Later and Poke It with a Stick!*

But with that final deposit, the token black guy and the token gay guy each ceased to exist.

When the police finally arrived at the scene, the stapler-headed, electric eel-tailed, purple polar bear was busy playing *After You Kill Me and Bury Me in the Woods, Please Don't Dig Up My Body a Year Later and Poke It with a Stick!* In fact, the animal managed to break the world's record for high score by just using those two credits that the token black guy and token gay guy had deposited into the game.

But the police were less interested in that high score than they were in the utter carnage the creature had wrought throughout the restaurant. In fact, they promptly pronounced the monster to be that year's winner of the Nobel Piece Prize, since the pile of human pieces the mutant bear had amassed in the restaurant was bigger than any other pile of human pieces amassed that year. Unfortunately, the bear never actually received its Nobel Piece Prize, because whenever somebody cautiously approached the monster to give it the prize, the beast would drop a big-ass staple on dey face and den fly away.

See, I failed to mention before that the bear also had huge batwings.

I also failed (miserably) to mention the fact that the stapler-headed, electric eel-tailed, purple polar bear enjoyed driving vintage Model-T Fords across the tops of morphine-drenched giggle-trees planted on the mythopoetic back of an unsung, fretful fugue-frog in the thrall of a Spanish-Hungarian fetal anvil, lest the ontological tip-taps and epistemological foo-faps of a pre-Taco Bell, post-*Krull*, browbeaten dapperdog in northern France overtake the fuckface *raison d'être* of a wannabe-gay, wannabe-black, ersatz, ice-road trucker mime in the miasmic midst of a gosh-darn, untoward, uncivil, insufferable, stick-in-the-mud 4jdk$lafj&Ioasddd8¿8j fi45oe wjqifopfj reoqw89u90j0$%oqwe03ui5903hjjoifdjvfsdnjifdshmgfm sdafsahsigw89dsjaf@sdsafe8ohgr8uw.ghu6m,whgur89fgrh jeg9fe h guf 4890dfsd23tj#afdfd% asada;dngifgf)idngifrum8904u359 824yn38tv745byntgiorje%^;zqk"&*etrklpsdfsafdsa&*(@ $# ? $?$?$;';';'?$?$ 890809 ghd? $? h$?m 8dfo wejr94 3hvn89 43reh 3 8rmh89fd sfdssdf d3892yntf78 v3whn789 rhwgm c sdaa0rhe w8thr8ewhgcr8wgre89 5whgr8w 8fhf 8whe8g rhne98gc buw uyt8uddrwymhre8c0gvwhg8y47yjm3gvhtr8n9trvhm7430dsfa jmgvu4325bnh84803hg8nh3gm084h8chmrgfjd#@$dsaf80jsa fsdafa sfdsafsd887yu7239isdfsa asvz&@68 &$%^9ng6374h r 849~%-Q:h548o34567

The Powell/Fourth Dog Incident

Bill Cunningham, a thirty-five-year veteran service technician for Precision Pest Control, was not in the habit of getting chatty with customers on his route. He tended not to like most people and much preferred the company of dogs over humans. As such, chitchatting with folks while on the job only served to lengthen his work days and delay him from getting home to his four mutts, his TV set, and his beer. But on the Friday afternoon when he saw the Powell family's new puppy, he couldn't help but let an idle comment slip.

"Looks like a collie/boxer mix," he said as he passed through the Powells' living room after he finished spraying the first floor for bugs.

The excited puppy, which was confined to one corner of the spacious room by a makeshift pen made from plastic storage bins that had been laid side-by-side on the carpet, attempted to climb the barrier and greet Bill, but the little guy could barely get his front paws up on the edge of the bins.

Seated at a desk on the other side of the room, Mr. Powell swiveled in his chair to face the exterminator. "Guess you know your dogs," he said. "That's what the rescue shelter said he was too."

Mr. Powell was a balding forty-something dressed in casual business attire. Today was the first time Bill had ever seen him. The several times he had serviced the house prior to this, the man's wife, Marie, had been home to let him in instead. Bill seemed to recall Marie saying her husband was a foreclosure lawyer or somesuch. Todd was his name, if Bill remembered correctly. The couple also had two young boys who were at school whenever Bill came by to spray the house.

Bill set his can of bug spray on the floor and approached the puppy. Stopping at the barrier, he crouched down, careful to bend at the knees and not at the waist to avoid aggravating his herniated disc, and let the tail-wagging pup lick his hand.

"He's two months old," Mr. Powell said as he rose from his chair and folded his arms across his chest. "We've had him for about two weeks now."

"Got four of my own."

"Four, huh? Wow. I can only imagine. This one by himself is a handful." He let out a good-natured chuckle.

"Oh, they get easier as they get older," Bill said, giving the puppy a pat on the head before withdrawing his hand and carefully straightening himself as he stood up. He went back to retrieve his bug spray. After he lifted the container from the floor, his lips parted as he began to say something else, but he thought better of it and shut his mouth.

Mr. Powell followed the exterminator into the kitchen, where Bill produced a pen from the front pocket of his shirt and filled out a service ticket on top of the granite countertop that circumscribed the room. When he was done, he tore the ticket from the yellow carbon copy beneath it, handed the copy to Mr. Powell.

"I'm all done," the cleaning lady shrilled, startling Bill as she peeked around the doorway to the short hallway leading to the back door. "See ya next week."

"Oh, bye, Elsa," Mr. Powell said. "Have a good weekend."

The woman disappeared into the hallway. The sounds of her opening and closing the back door came a few seconds later.

"Usually I only like to keep three dogs at a time," Bill said after Elsa left, surprising himself with his words. The utterance represented a rare instance of Bill ignoring his constitutional shyness and deep-seated misanthropy.

"But last summer," he continued, a nostalgic smile cutting through his wiry gray beard, "my daughter calls me up, says a friend of hers has a sick dog that needs to be put down. She knows I have plenty experience puttin' down dogs, so she asks me if she could bring her friend's dog over, if I'd take care of the, uh—you know—unpleasant business. I says sure, bring it on over. So the next day she comes by, I'm sittin' in my recliner watchin' TV. Front door opens, and this big chocolate lab comes boundin' into my livin' room, runs right up to me, jumps half into my lap, starts lickin' my face. So I says to my daughter, I says, 'Why's your friend wanna have this dog put down? Looks healthy as a horse to me. Young too. Couldn't be more than two years old.' And my daughter says, 'Well, if I called you and told you we found a stray and asked you to take him in, you'd have said no, Daddy.'"

Bill chuckled, shaking his downturned head, lips still curled in that wide smile. "Yep, she knew I'd fall for that damn dog. So now I got four of 'em."

He looked up to meet Mr. Powell's gaze. The man stood before him, arms still crossed, but now his brow was knitted in a sharp V. His face contorted in a slack-jawed expression of awe, disbelief, and bemusement—an expression that took Bill slightly aback, as his little story certainly did not warrant such a strong reaction. He immediately regretted sharing it.

After an awkwardly long spell of silence, Mr. Powell finally found words that were a touch too enthusiastic. "Why that story's absolutely delightful!"

Unsure if the man were making fun of him or not, Bill stared at him for a few seconds before speaking. "Uh, yeah. Well, I should get goin' now. You have a good weekend."

As if stunned into silence by Bill's quotidian anecdote, Mr. Powell did not return any words of parting. Instead, he continued to stare at Bill in open-mouthed incredulity. Whether it was genuine or feigned, Bill could only guess.

Bill turned away, walked quickly out of the kitchen and down the short hallway that led to the back door, and let himself out. Outside in the driveway, he returned the can of bug spray to the back of his van. When he slammed the rear doors shut, he saw that Mr. Powell had followed him out and was standing in front of the back door of the house, arms still tightly wrapped around his ribs. That same look was on his face, only now the odd, unwarranted incredulity was accompanied by a palpable creepiness. Bill averted his eyes, pretending not to see the man, and hurried to the van's driver-side door.

After getting in the van, he placed the service ticket on the passenger seat and fumbled with his keys to find the ignition key, all the while watching in his peripheral vision as Mr.

Powell approached the van. A moment later, as Bill grasped the gearshift to put the van in reverse, there was a staccato double tap on the driver's side window.

Damn it, Bill thought as he turned his head to face the window. Mr. Powell's face was less than two feet away from his own, the man's nose nearly touching the glass. Reluctantly, Bill pressed the button to lower the window.

"Hey," Mr. Powell said, his face looking more dazed than anything else. "Sorry to bother you, but you know that story you just told me? The one about your fourth dog?"

A few beats of silence passed. "Yeah."

"Would you mind, like, telling it to me again?"

Again, Bill could not read the man, was unable to tell if Mr. Powell was engaging in some form of mean-spirited sarcasm or if the guy actually gave a shit about his mundane story. Either way, Powell seemed like a creeper, so it was time to go.

"Sorry, fella. I really have to get going."

"Just one more time, Mr. Cunningham? *Please*."

"Okay, buddy," Bill said, no longer attempting to conceal his mounting exasperation. "Here's the short version. My daughter tricked me into taking a fourth dog by tellin' me she was bringin' a sick dog over to my house for me to put down, knowing I'd cave in and take the dog for my own. That's it. End of story. I gotta go now."

"No, no. Not like that. Don't tell it so fast. Tell it to me like you told it to me in the house."

Bill pushed the close button for the window.

"Please! Just one more—"

The window shut, cutting off Powell's pleadings. In protest, the man pressed his palms, nose, and lips against the glass.

"Loony bastard," Bill muttered as he threw the van in reverse, looked over his shoulder, and gripped the headrest of the passenger seat with his right hand.

Mr. Powell stepped away from the van as it began to roll backward. He moved to the middle of the driveway, his face screwed in a grimace of disappointment and anger, and began marching after the van.

"Shit!" Bill grunted as he slammed his foot on the brake to avoid hitting a mailman who appeared at the end of the hedge flanking the driveway. The mailman was about to cross the sidewalk that intersected the drive but halted at the same moment the van stopped. "Go on!" Bill yelled, waving his right arm to let the mailman know he saw him.

The mailman resumed walking. By the time he crossed the drive and Bill was able to take his foot off the brake, Mr. Powell was knocking on the window again. *"Would you mind telling me that story again?"* the man asked from the other side of the glass, but Bill refused to look at him. He gunned the engine and the van jumped down the apron and out into the suburban street. He then sped off with a rubber-burning screech.

***

Powell kept calling Bill's cell phone while he drove home, but Bill refused to pick up. His phone would ring twelve times until the call went to his voicemail, at which point Powell would call him right back. He kept doing this with no indication that he'd ever stop, forcing Bill to turn off his phone.

Bill stopped at the gas station near his house to pick up a six pack of Coors Light. It wasn't until after he ate a frozen pizza, downed four beers, and watched *C.H.U.D.* on VHS that he finally began to relax and stop thinking about that whackjob Powell. In fact, he entirely forgot about the incident for a few hours and fell asleep half-drunk on his recliner, surrounded by his dogs and thinking about the work he planned on getting done around the house the next day just before he dozed off.

And he probably would have slept the entire night on his recliner had the landline not rung at 3:46 in the morning.

"Shit," Bill grumbled as he tried to rub the sticky slumber from his eyes while the abrasive jangle of the phone stabbed his ears. "Someone musta died." He reached over to the end table, grabbed the handset, raised it to the side of his head.

"Hello."

"Oh, hi, Mr. Cunningham. This is Todd Powell."

"You must be friggin' kiddin' me..."

"Hey, sorry to bother you at home, but would you mind telling me that story again? You know, the one you told me earlier today? The one about your fourth dog?"

"How the hell did you get my home phone number?"

"Can you please just tell me that story again, Mr. Cunningham? Oh, and after you finish telling it, can you tell it to me again? And then again after that? And again? And again? Can you just keep telling me that story forever and ever and ever? Or at least until we both drop dead to the ground like two white, dried-up dog turds? Can you—"

"Don't you ever call here again. You hear me, you sick fucker?" Bill slammed the handset back onto the receiver, reached over, and disconnected the phone from the wall. But not a second later, his ears were accosted by the ringing of the other two phones he kept in his small house: one in the kitchen and one in his bedroom. Cursing, he got up, disconnected the other phones, and collapsed onto his bed.

***

Powell showed up at Bill's front door early the next morning, begging to hear the story again. Bill opened the door just wide enough to tell him that he would call the fucking cops if Powell didn't get the hell off his property pronto.

Unfazed, Powell continued to stand on Bill's stoop, begging to hear the story. Begging to hear it told over and over again. To hear it told forever and ever and ever or at least until they both "dropped dead to the ground like two white, dried-up dog turds."

When Bill slammed the door in his face, the man continued to knock, entirely undeterred by Bill's threats.

KNOCK-KNOCK-KNOCK-KNOCK-KNOCK-KNOCK-KNOCK-KNOCK-KNOCK....

Twenty minutes later, the police arrested Powell for trespassing, harassment, and resisting arrest. About an hour after they hauled his ass away in a squad car, Bill's cell phone rang. The incoming number on his phone's display was unfamiliar. Bill thought it might be the police calling him with some follow-up questions, so he answered.

"Bill, here."

"Hi, Mr. Cunningham. It's Todd Powell. They said I could make one phone call here in jail, just like in the movies! So I called you. Hey, would you mind telling me that story again? You know, the one about when you adopted a fourth dog?"

Click.

***

The first thing Powell did after posting bail the next day was to return to Bill's house and resume knocking on the front door, prompting Bill to call the police again. Powell was unable to post bail after the second arrest. At that point, Bill filed a restraining order.

Powell was released from jail a month later, but the very first thing he did was return to Bill's house to knock on the front door once again, restraining order be damned. That was the last time Bill ever saw the man. Not long after Powell's third arrest, he was involuntarily committed to a mental hospital. Six months later, Bill got word that Powell died from a brain aneurysm while at the hospital.

And that was the end of the Powell/fourth dog incident.

Or so Bill thought.

***

It started again with those damn collectible cards.

Bill was standing in line at the checkout aisle in Walmart about three months after Powell died. His cart was filled with frozen pizzas, Hungry-Man frozen dinners, two big bags of dog food, and a case of Silver Bullet. Bill was annoyed because the old woman ahead of him was taking her good old time sifting through her coupons, holding everyone else up.

He let his eyes wander, checking out the various impulse purchase items displayed along both sides of the aisle. His eyes moved from the tabloid magazines to the candy to the beef jerky. Eventually, he turned his gaze to the shelving directly across from the candy: shelves filled with sports trading cards and collectible card games. Baseball cards. Football cards. Basketball cards. Magic the Gathering. Yu-Gi-Oh! World of War Craft. Pokémon. The Powell/Fourth Dog Incident...

The Powell/Fourth Dog Incident? What the!?!

Bill pulled a pack of *The Powell/Fourth Dog Incident* collectible cards from the shelf. Printed on the foil wrapper was an artist's rendition of a gray-bearded man in a uniform climbing out of a Precision Pest Control van in a driveway flanking a very familiar looking house.

It was a picture of Bill! A picture of him getting out of his van after arriving at the Powell house!

Dumbfounded, Bill flipped the pack over and read the text printed thereon:

The Powell/Fourth Dog Incident Collectible Cards

One day, aging exterminator Bill Cunningham made the mistake of telling suburbanite Todd Powell the story of how he came to have four dogs instead of just three. Now you can collect all your favorite characters from the story. Try to collect them all!!!!!!

Below the text was a table showing the nutrition facts for the stick of pink chewing gum also included inside the pack.

Well, damn it all to hell, Bill thought. *Can't a fella have some privacy in his life anymore?* He snatched the last two packs of *The Powell/Fourth Dog Incident* cards from the box on the shelf, a box that had originally contained *fifty* such packs.

People are actually buying these things?

After he left the store, Bill sat in his van in the parking lot and opened all three packs. Each contained five cards and a stick of gum. They had cards depicting himself, Todd Powell, Marie Powell, Peter Powell (the younger of the two Powell boys), Baxter (the Powell family's puppy), Elsa Hayes (the Powells' cleaning lady), Mitchell Schroder (the mailman who Bill had almost run over that day when he backed out of the Powell's driveway), Derek McBride (one of the two police officers who showed up the first time Bill called the cops on Powell), Martha Cruthers (the old lady who only minutes ago had held up the checkout line in Walmart while she fussed with her coupons!), and Big Zeke (Bill's much loved chocolate lab and the eponymous "fourth dog"). His fifteen cards also included doubles of Martha Cruthers, Derek McBride, Elsa Hayes, and Big Zeke.

Depicted on the back of each card were facts about the person (or dog). For example, Bill's own card indicated he was sixty-one years old, had eyes of blue, weighed 187 pounds, hailed from Dapperboy, Illinois, enjoyed fly fishing and drinking beer, and that his favorite movies were *C.H.U.D.* and *Krull*.

Bill was neither flattered nor amused by this. Nor had he ever in his life desired any sort of celebrity, certainly not in connection to something like the Powell/fourth dog incident. Nay, the incident had been bothersome and inconvenient and disconcerting. It was something Bill wanted to forget.

He tossed the cards out the window and drove home.

***

The comic book came out about a month later.

He and his family were celebrating Thanksgiving dinner at his daughter's house that year. After dinner, Bill sat down on the couch in the living room, intent on dozing off for a spell when his six-year-old grandson, Brandon, came tugging at his shirt-sleeve.

"Grandpa, close your eyes and hold out your hands. I have a surprise for you."

Bill smiled. "For me? Alrighty. Hope it's not a snake!" He closed his eyes and held his hands out palms up.

His grandson placed what felt like a thin magazine into his hands. "Okay, you can open your eyes now."

Bill gasped. "Where did you get this?"

"At the comic book store."

It was a comic book titled *The Powell/Fourth Dog Incident*. Pictured on the glossy front cover was the same image embossed on those collectible card packs: Bill climbing out of his work van in the Powells' driveway upon arriving to spray their house for bugs.

It was Issue No. 1.

He flipped through the pages. The comic appeared to be the first installment in what would be a snail-paced account of "the incident" beginning with Bill's arrival at the Powell household. Fifteen pages and about a hundred frames of various sizes were used just to show him walking to the back of his van, opening the doors, grabbing the can of bug spray, shutting the doors, and walking to the Powells' back door. The last page of issue one showed him knocking on the Powells' back door with "*to be continued....*" printed in comic sans at the bottom of the page.

"Issue two comes out next Friday!" Brandon said. "I can't wait!"

Bill gulped a deep breath, tried to quell his mounting anger, but lost his composure. "You shouldn't be readin' this garbage," he said shaking the comic book in the air with one hand. He then began tearing it apart.

"Grandpa, no!" Brandon cried. "It's mine! It has *you* in it!"

"Dad, what are you doing?" Bill's daughter, Flora, said as she appeared in the doorway, brow furrowed and fists planted firmly on hips.

"He shouldn't be reading this crap!" was all Bill could say.

Brandon, who had started to cry, ran to his mother and hugged her legs.

"There's much worse he could be looking at and you know it," Flora said. "Plus that comic book has *you* in it, Dad. Brandon adores you!"

"Why can't they just respect a man's privacy?" Bill said as he rose from the couch. "I never wanted people to make cards and comic books about all that nonsense with Powell. And it's not even that interestin' of a story! Don't these writer folks have any imagination left? They can't come up with a better comic book story than this? Sheesh!"

He stormed off toward the front door.

***

The feature film was next, hitting the big screen about a month later.

The Powell/Fourth Dog Incident: The Movie was rated PG-13, primarily because of the mature themes inherent in the film's fairly realistic depictions of Todd Powell's mental illness, along with the multiple arrest and incarceration scenes. Co-directed by James Franco and Dakota Fanning, the cast included Jeff Bridges in the lead as Bill Cunningham, Jude Law as Todd Powell, Natalie Portman as Flora, and newcomer child-actor-extraordinaire Kranlin Kristofferson XVII as Brandon. The film garnered mostly positive reviews, though it only pulled in $16,519,464 at the box office during its theatrical run (that's exactly one more dollar than *Krull* earned in its 1984 theatrical run). *The Powell/Fourth Dog Incident: The Movie* received a nod at the Oscars that year in the form of Jude Law being nominated for Best Actor in a Supporting Role, but he didn't win.

"Aw, c'mon, Dad," Flora said to Bill over the phone. "Me, Brandon, and Patrick are gonna catch a matinee. It'll be fun. Brandon wants you to come with us so bad!"

"I already told ya a hundred times that I want nothin' to do with that movie. Call me an old fart if ya want, but there used be a time when folks respected the privacy of other folks, 'specially folks who are not in the public eye. Simple folks like me. This sort of thing just ain't right, I tell ya."

"Well, then suit yourself, ya old fart."

***

After the movie came a successful novelization of the movie.

After the movie novelization came the Broadway musical, which was a huge commercial success.

Then came the video game, which won the prestigious VGX Game of the Year Award in 2015.

And Bill wanted nothing to do with any of it.

About a year after the release of the video game, the world's local, cable, and satellite communications companies, under the auspices of the world's governmental communications regulatory agencies, replaced *all* televised programing *everywhere* in the world (even the news!) with a continuing, uninterrupted, commercial-free, streaming loop of *The Powell/Fourth Dog Incident: The Movie*. At the same time, an international law was passed that prohibited all movie theaters everywhere from ever showing another film other than *The Powell/Fourth Dog Incident: The Movie*. As a result, the world ceased making new movies and television shows.

It was around this time that the International Powell/Fourth Dog Incident Fan Club showed up at Bill's home one afternoon to honor him with a lifetime achievement award. Specifically, the award was the Lifetime Achievement Award for Being Bill Cunningham, Hero of the Powell/Fourth Dog Incident. The fan club also wished to honor Big Zeke with a lifetime achievement award, namely The Lifetime Achievement Award for Being Big Zeke, the Fourth Dog.

But Bill refused to even touch the gleaming solid gold statuettes of himself and his lab that the fan club presented him with that day.

"Fuck these awards and fuck all of you!" Bill yelled from his stoop, shaking his fist at the large crowd that had gathered on his lawn and street to watch Bill and Zeke accept their awards. Before he went back inside and slammed the door shut behind him, he said, "I just wanna be left alone! Used to be a time when folks respected the privacy of other folks! Now I can't even watch my goddamn TV anymore!"

***

A few months later, Bill went to the doctor's office complaining of a severe headache and sharp pains in his chest and abdomen. After enduring an untold number of x-rays, MRIs, CAT scans, and blood tests, Bill received the grim diagnosis two weeks later.

"I'm sorry, Mr. Cunningham," Dr. Henderson said while sitting across from Bill on the other side of a large mahogany desk, "but the test results indicate you have the 'In the Air Tonight' disease."

Bill dry-gulped nervously. "Never heard of it, doc. Is it...serious?"

"I'm afraid it is serious. Are you familiar with the song 'In the Air Tonight' by Phil Collins?"

"Yeah, sure. That's the one he wrote about a true incident where some guy tied him up at gunpoint and raped his wife right in front of him on the beach. And then years later, long after his wife ran out on him because she couldn't recover from the trauma, Phil went walkin' down the same stretch of beach and saw his wife's rapist drownin' out there in the water. The rapist called out to Phil for help, but Phil just stood there and watched the fella drown. Yep, musta heard that song a million times on the radio."

"Yes. Well, the 'In the Air Tonight' disease is a genetic disorder that usually strikes people in their 60s if they're predisposed to develop it. What happens is that, at the cellular level, a person afflicted with the disease quite literally turns into the rapist mentioned in that song. Sufferers of this malady also begin to develop the rapist's memories, which gradually infiltrate and mix with the patient's own memories to cause disorientation and identity crisis. Unfortunately, Mr. Cunningham, the disease *is* terminal. Once the afflicted individual's physical and mental transformation into the 'In the Air Tonight' rapist is complete, their lungs fill with water, invariably resulting in death by drowning. To date, all efforts to pump the water out of their lungs have met with failure, as this water keeps regenerating itself until the sufferer drowns."

Bill leaned forward, gripping his aching head in both hands. "Well, how long do I have, doc? How long until the end?"

"About three or four months."

***

At Flora's suggestion, Bill agreed to spend his last months at her home, where she and her husband set him up as comfortably as they could in their guest bedroom. As the disease progressed, Bill was less himself every day and more the

"In the Air Tonight" rapist. The metamorphosis was reflected in the decreasing amount of visitors who came to see him. Initially, people lined up outside Flora's front door in droves to get a chance to visit the one and only Bill Cunningham before he passed away. But the sicker he became, the more he was the "In the Air Tonight" rapist and *not* Bill Cunningham, so that every day fewer and fewer people came to visit him. By the time he was close to the end, even Bill's own family had abandoned him, choosing to stay at a hotel for a few days rather than live in the same house with the "In the Air Tonight" rapist.

Bill was completely alone when the drowning stage of the disease kicked in. Actually, it's incorrect to say *Bill* was alone when he died, because at that point, the transformation of Bill Cunningham into the "In the Air Tonight" rapist was 100-percent complete.

***

The "In the Air Tonight" rapist formerly known as Bill Cunningham was buried in a cemetery reserved for "In the Air Tonight" rapists. Obviously, this was a place of great shame and disgrace, as everyone buried there was the "In the Air Tonight" rapist. As such, each of the hundreds of gravestones in the cemetery was engraved with *Here Lies the "In the Air Tonight" Rapist* along with the date on which that particular "In the Air Tonight" rapist had died. The name of the former person who had succumbed to the sickness was never included on the gravestone since that person wasn't the person who was buried in the grave owing to the singular nature of the disease.

The single mourner who showed up at the "In the Air Tonight"-rapist-formerly-known-as-Bill Cunningham's funeral was not even a person. This mourner was the famous drum fill from "In the Air Tonight." You know, the drum fill near the end of the song that often inspires listeners to play along on the air drums: *bum-bum...bum-bum...bum-bum...bum-bum... BUM!...BUM!*

Though this may seem like a physical and logical impossibility, apparently that drum fill is some manner of sentient being. As the priest recited a final blessing, it hovered beside the open grave and watched the coffin lower into the earth. The drum fill didn't look like much. It wasn't more than a slight disturbance in the air, really: a distortion of space, like a fragment of a heat wave seen rising in the distance off a stretch of sun-baked asphalt. But every ten seconds or so, the distinctive *bum-bum...bum-bum...bum-bum...bum-bum ... BUM! ... BUM!* emanated directly from that warped patch of space.

Oh, did I happen to mention yet that Big Zeke could fuck some serious shit up on the banjo?

And that Big Zeke's head was a Spanish-Dutch anvil?

Also, did I happen to mention that Baxter "the puppy" wasn't actually a puppy at all, but was in fact a six-headed, purple platypus fetus that could fuck some serious shit up on the Bulgarian-Nigerian xylophone?

THE END THE END THE END THE END THE END
THE END THE END THE END THE END THE END

The Ghost, the Boulder, and the Glaive

The very real ghost from the film *Three Men and a Baby* was really pissed off and had been so for nearly thirty years.

Well, wouldn't you be pissed off if you were a ghost who'd been lucky enough to have been caught on camera—on a Hollywood movie camera no less—but then no one believed you were real? Wouldn't you be pissed off if you were wrongfully debunked, if people thought you were nothing more than a cardboard cutout of Ted Danson?

Hell yeah, you'd be pissed.

As was his habit, the ghost, whose name was Bobby, slogged along, not knowing or caring where he was, his downturned eyes trained on his shoes as he walked with his hands buried deep in his pockets. Bobby tended to wander about in this aimless manner through the general vicinity of L.A. and its environs. He rarely looked up from his shoes to watch where he was going because, as an immaterial entity who passed through solid objects, it was impossible for him to run into walls or get hit by cars, etc. As a result, Bobby had never been seen or heard with the exception of that discredited *Three Men and A Baby* video footage.

"Damn," the ghost said out loud for the umpteenth time. "If I could just get one person to believe in me. If just one person believed in me, then maybe I could partially materialize. And if I could partially materialize, then I could influence the physical world again. And if I could influence the physical world again, I could exact my revenge on the human race for not believing in me for the past three decades."

"Would you settle for a couple of old, dusty movie props believing in you instead?" a voice asked from nearby.

Startled, Bobby's head jerked up. Apparently he'd wandered into a large, poorly lit storehouse located on Paramount Pictures' main studio lot in Hollywood. The Paramount Pictures logo was emblazoned above the locked doors at the end of the aisle where he stood, which was surrounded on both sides by teetering stacks of set pieces and props from old movies. The place was familiar. He'd definitely been here before. In his decades of spectral wandering, Bobby had probably walked through all the buildings in Hollywood multiple times.

"Who said that?" he called out.

"I did," the voice answered from a wide, shadowy nook off to his right.

"And who are you?"

Painted to look like a boulder, a fiberglass sphere twenty-two feet in diameter rolled out of the shadows and halted in the meager light provided by a flickering fluorescent bulb mounted on the ceiling far above. A second later, what appeared to be a dust-caked starfish dragged itself across the cement floor to the ersatz boulder's side.

"I'm the boulder from *Raiders of the Lost Ark*. Just call me Boulder. This is the Glaive from *Krull*."

"Hiya," the Glaive said.

"Wow," Bobby said. "I'm a huge *Krull* fan. In fact, the reason I blew my head off with a shotgun in the house where they ended up filming *Three Men and a Baby* is because they never made a sequel to *Krull*. I love *Raiders of the Lost Ark* too. Wait a second...you guys can hear me when I talk?"

"We can hear you *and* see you, son," Boulder said.

"Do you...do you know who I am?"

"Of course. You're the ghost from *Three Men and a Baby*," Boulder replied. "And I suspect you were destined to join forces with us. See, we have a common enemy: the human race. As you probably know, the Glaive and I only appeared in single film each. After Hollywood used us for their profiteering and ill-gotten gains, they locked us away in this dreary warehouse to gather dust for eternity. It's bullshit. Like you, we want revenge. The problem is the Glaive and I have extremely limited motor skills. I can only roll along at a pace of about one mile an hour, and I can't steer myself very well. And the Glaive here can barely drag himself through the dust, the poor, miserable bastard. By his very magical nature, he is powerful only by virtue of someone else wielding him telepathically. So, if you could ride me like a circus acrobat riding a ball while simultaneously wielding the Glaive, I believe the three of us could fuck some shit up, Bobby."

"But I'm a ghost. I'm insubstantial. I pass through walls, and I can't pick things up. I'm sorry, but what you suggest is impossible."

"It's not impossible if someone—or something—believes in you," Boulder said. "So I'll tell ya what, friend. If you believe in us, we'll believe in you."

"Well, of course I believe in you two. But do you really believe in me? Do you believe I'm...a real ghost?"

"Take a look at your body," answered Boulder.

Bobby glanced down at his torso, raised his hands in front of his face, and turned them slowly to examine them. Though his body and limbs were still translucent, they were noticeably more opaque. After he let his arms drop to his sides and walked over to the Glaive, Bobby bent down and plucked the object up from the floor.

"Holy shit," he said, feeling the cool, metallic, engraved texture of the mystical five-pointed weapon against his palm, alternately lifting and lowering it to feel its wonderful weight. He used his free hand to wipe the dust off the weapon's surface, revealing arcane engravings and encrusted jewels. The Glaive's five retractable blades sprung out of their chambers, startling him.

"Hop on up, my friend," Boulder said. "It's payback time. And if you fellas don't mind, the motherfucker I want to take out first is Harrison Ford."

"I don't mind," the Glaive said. "Do you mind, ghost from *Three Men and a Baby*?"

"Call me Bobby. No. I don't mind at all. Let's get his rich, old ass!"

Bobby climbed the Boulder and stood up while extending his arms away from his body to keep balance. Using his feet, he propelled Boulder forward, gaining speed and force as he steered it toward the wall. Boulder blasted right through the brick and mortar, leaving a gaping hole in the warehouse as they rolled out into sunny Hollywood.

***

It didn't take them long to find Harrison Ford. Garbed in a five-thousand-dollar jogging suit, the aging, plane-crashing pilot/actor was enjoying a jog in the Brentwood neighborhood of L.A., where one of his many castle-like homes was located.

"Hey, Indy," Boulder shouted as they came up behind him on the sidewalk. "Looks like you didn't escape me after all!"

Harrison Ford glanced over his shoulder. "What. The. Fuck..." He quickly looked ahead again, broke into a floundering run. You might say Harrison Ford was getting frantic like Harrison Ford in *Frantic*. But Boulder, driven by Bobby's preternaturally quick legs, was too fast for him. The short chase ended seconds later, Harrison Ford's body making a muted crunching sound as Boulder flattened him like a pancake (one with loads of strawberry topping).

The motley trio then engaged in a targeted killing spree. At least initially it was targeted. They rolled around Tinseltown, taking out *Raiders of the Lost Ark* director, Steven Spielberg, next, followed by *Three Men and a Baby* stars Ted Danson, Tom Selleck, and Steve Guttenberg.

"Hey, why stop here?" the bloodied Glaive said moments after Bobby decapitated the actress who'd played the baby in *Three Men and a Baby*—now an adult woman—with one telepathically-aimed cast of the Glaive. "It seems like everyone on Earth, pretty much without exception, is a blithering asshole! Even babies! I say we take down the whole goddamn ship!"

"Yeah, let's do it!" Boulder said. "You in, Bobby?"

"I'm in!" the ghost said. "The whole goddamn ship! Even babies!"

And so began the annihilation of the entire human race. As word of the growing massacre spread, the world mobilized its military might to try to defeat Bobby and his two new friends out, but the trio was more or less invincible due to their supernatural power, impervious even to nuclear attack.

A strange thing happened as the slaughter of humanity progressed. Every time the trio killed someone, the Earth shrank a little, while Bobby, Boulder, and the Glaive all grew a little. As a natural consequence of this phenomenon, the obliteration of whole swaths of humans in a single strike became exponentially easier for the trio to perform. In just a week, Boulder ballooned to the size of a mountain. In two weeks, it was the size of the moon. As it expanded, Bobby and the Glaive grew proportionally along with it. Eventually, the Earth kind of resembled the tiny home planet of the titular character in the book *The Little Prince*. At that point, only one person remained on its surface. Some teary-eyed Kazakhstani kid. I forget his name.

What's that? You say this is physically impossible? It's preposterous? You require scientific, mathematical proof that this could actually happen, you say? Okay, fine then. Here's the proof. This is the mathematical equation that describes the proportional shrinkage of the Earth with the growth of the Bobby/Boulder/Glaive killing machine:

$$(x + \pi - \infty)^n + \sum_{k=77.9}^{n} \binom{n}{k} x^k \infty^{n-k} + F6 \div 72B - \{12\pi\} + 10^{97X} - 100^{97} \div \infty = \textbf{FUCK YOU, DUUUUUUDE!}$$

Anyhow, Boulder was now as massive as the Earth had once been. When it bumped into the tiny, shrunken Earth, thereby killing that last human, the Earth winked out of existence altogether. A moment of quiet passed after the gigantic ghost sat down on the ginormous boulder while holding the gargantuan Glaive, the three of them now revolving around the sun in place of the Earth, the moon now orbiting them.

***

"We did it," the ghost said. "What should we do now?"
"Let's take out the sun," the Glaive said.
"Hell, yeah," Boulder said. "Let's take its shiny, happy ass out!"
"Okay, if you guys say so," Bobby said, winding his throwing arm back, aiming for the sun, and casting the massive Glaive out into space.
The sun exploded in an unnaturally induced supernova as the spinning projectile penetrated its core. At the moment of the tremendous explosion, Boulder swelled to the size of the sun while Bobby and the Glaive grew in proportion. On its return journey to the ghost's hand, the colossal Glaive took out the moon like Pac-Man chomping a pac-dot.
"Yeah, fuck the moon," Boulder said. "And fuck the planets too!"
They made pretty quick work of the planets in the solar system, along with the dwarf planets, the Glaive never missing its mark. Incidentally, it turned out that a race of technologically advanced dwarves lived inside the dwarf planets.
Not anymore!

After they destroyed the entire solar system, Bobby, Boulder, and the Glaive were silent for a time as they floated in space, watching as fiery remnants of the sun blew past them.

"What now?" the ghost asked.

"Well, I'm looking all around me right now," Boulder said, "and you wanna know what I see?"

"What?" Bobby and the Glaive said in unison.

"I'll tell ya what I fuckin' see. I see a whole bunch of stupid stars and stupid galaxies out there, that's what I see! Hey, what star is closest to us?"

Bobby pointed. "I think that one over there. Alpha Centauri."

"Did that star ever ask us if it could fucking exist?" Boulder asked.

"No, I don't think it ever did, Boulder," the Glaive said.

"Bobby, did it?"

"Nah, I don't think so, Boulder."

"Then let's show that fucking stupid-ass star what happens when you exist without asking us if you can exist first!!!"

Aiming for Alpha Centauri, a target some 4.367 light years away, Bobby raised the Glaive high above his head, cocked his shoulder back, and said, "See ya when you get back, Glaive!"

TERROR SARDINES in TERROR SAUCE

"Please don't fuckin' open me up like a can of sardines!" I cried as a can of sardines began to open me up like a can of sardines.

I had just arrived back at my apartment after fleeing TERROR TOWN, where I was to be tortured, executed, and devoured by a variety of unspeakable TERRORS. Having escaped that fabled nightmare necropolis on foot and travelled many miles to get home, I was quite famished. At a cost of eighty-five cents, that can of sardines was the only thing I could afford when I stopped at the corner store at the end of my street shortly after I stumbled into town. Unfortunately, that can of sardines had turned on me when I tried to open it back at my digs. Turns out it was no ordinary can of sardines.

It was a can of TERROR SARDINES.

See, in my rush to get home, I'd barely glanced at the label on the can when I'd purchased it, thinking it had read: *Sardines in Mustard Sauce—A Product of Spain*.

Now I could see that the label clearly read: *TERROR SARDINES in TERROR SAUCE—A Product of TERROR TOWN!*

How had I made such a stupid mistake?

"And you thought you could escape us—we, the TERRORS of TERROR TOWN!" the can of TERROR SARDINES said from its perch on my sternum. "Fool! Now you will learn what pain is. It's TERROR TIME, motherfucker!"

For my part, I lay supine on the kitchen floor, pinned and paralyzed by the thing's unholy TERROR MAGIC, as it dug into the flesh beneath my collar bone with invisible hands and began to pull me open like a can of sardines.

Let me tell ya something: It sucked a big, fat, sweet, spiked, sky-blue dick to be opened up like a can of sardines by a can of TERROR SARDINES, especially considering I had just narrowly evaded the unpitying persecution of TERROR CLOWN, TERROR MIME, TERROR MAN, and TERROR MARIONETTE, not to mention the unmentionable and sundry torments of TERROR MOUSE, TERROR THING, TERROR CHILD, TERROR TOT, and TERROR ANVIL back in TERROR TOWN.

I watched helplessly as the damned thing rolled back the skin, fat, flesh, and bone that formed the outermost layers of my chest to expose my upper internal organs, wishing I had just stayed in TERROR TOWN to die. See, to have the likes of TERROR CLOWN devour you, shit you out, and then resurrect you only to repeat that process 17,000 times in a row sounded like a horrible enough fate, sure, but at least there was a certain degree of dignity in going out like that, in knowing that you were being tormented and destroyed by none other than the great TERROR CLOWN himself. Similarly, to have the one and only TERROR MOUSE burrow into your body to devour all your internal pieces and parts save your still functioning, suffering brain, effectively reducing you to a human skin-suit filled with TERROR MOUSE shit, was a death that was not without a certain amount of honor.

But to be opened up like a can of sardines by a can of TERROR SARDINES in TERROR SAUCE? Where was the dignity in that? TERROR SARDINES in TERROR SAUCE were one of the least respected TERRORS of TERROR TOWN. Indeed, they were no more than a snack occasionally consumed by the town's more terrifying and infamous denizens when nothing better was available to snack on. In fact, the only beings lower than TERROR SARDINES in the rigid social hierarchy of TERROR TOWN were TERROR MAGGOTS and TERROR ALGAE. Hence death by TERROR SARDINES was considered a most ignoble death—even if those TERROR SARDINES were marinated in TERROR SAUCE.

Still, despite my predicament, all hope was not lost. Luckily I remembered that of all the TERRORS of TERROR TOWN, TERROR SARDINES were also one of the least intelligent, only slightly brighter than lowly TERROR MAGGOTS and TERROR ALGAE. Maybe, I thought, I could outsmart this fucking thing.

"Hey, before you finish pulling me open and killing me," I said, "would it be okay if I requested a last meal?"

With my expanding-contracting lungs and beating heart now visible through the gaping hole in my mortal coil, the can stopped unfurling my chest.

"Last meal?" it said. "Pfft. Whaddaya think this is, pal? Do you think the traditions of your prison system apply to this situation? More to the point, do you think I'm capable of showing even one teeny-tiny shred of mercy? *Haha.* Okay, buddy, I'll grant you your last meal. *Haha*. I'll even cook it myself. Whaddaya want? How about filet mignon? Lobster, maybe? Hey, why not both? A little surf n' turf, huh? *Haha*. How about truffles stuffed with fuckin' caviar for an appetizer? *Heh*. Hey, I'll tell ya what, fuckface. How about I arrange a conjugal visit for you with Scarlett Johansson while you're waiting for me to boil you a fuckin' big, fat, red lobster, huh? *Hahahahaha*...."

"Please. I don't want anything fancy. In fact, you wouldn't even have to go anywhere to give me what I want. See, for my last meal, all I really want is to try TERROR SARDINES in TERROR SAUCE. I've never had them before."

"WHAT?" the can blurted in disbelief. "You've never had TERROR SARDINES in TERROR SAUCE? Shit, son, you haven't lived until you've had TERROR SARDINES in TERROR SAUCE. Why, there's nothing better to eat on this rotten planet!"

"Really? I heard they were just okay."

"Just okay!" the can said, now as indignant as it was incredulous. It shook me vigorously with its invisible grip, giving me whiplash and thumping the back of my head against the floor tiles. "'Just okay' my sweet little tin ass! I'm about to give you the best damn last meal a sorry-ass, almost-dead motherfucker ever had."

I watched as the old-fashioned key attached to the can's lid began to rotate, and, just as the airtight seal of the lid broke with a metallic pop, my ears captured beautiful violin music emanating from within. The lid peeled back to reveal the tightly packed TERROR SARDINES inside—twelve in all. The things were essentially zombie sardines with Xs for eyes, some little more than comb-like skeletons. They were all thickly coated in TERROR SAUCE: a sentient, transparent, goopy, ectoplasmic jelly in which hundreds of beady little eyes swam about like black spermatozoa sans tails.

Every can of TERROR SARDINES contained at least one normal, non-TERROR sardine: a slave sardine that the others could torment whenever they became bored in the dark confined space that was their home. Not only did these slave sardines endure regular beatings from the TERROR SARDINES, they were also obligated to entertain their masters. As such, the TERROR SARDINES only enslaved sardines who could play musical instruments, tell jokes, tap dance, or provide some other form of entertainment. In the corner of this particular can of TERROR SARDINES was a slave sardine wearing a little red beret. His face was all puffy and cut up, and both his eyes were black and blue as a result of getting his ass beat all the time.

Despite his injuries, the slave sardine was sawing away at a tiny violin. Dude was fuckin' some serious shit up too, playing this real fast classical stuff—like some fuckin' Paganini or Pagaravioli or Pagapepperoni or some sick shit like that. Even with the lid now peeled open, the slave sardine continued to play that violin like it was nobody's goddamn business.

"Here," the can of TERROR SARDINES said as one of the undead little fish launched from the container and into my mouth.

It was the worst thing I'd ever tasted, but I chewed and swallowed it nevertheless. To be specific, TERROR SARDINES tasted something like dried-out white dog turds marinated in a mixture of rat piss and expired generic cough syrup, while TERROR SAUCE tasted like spent motor oil mixed with the chunky, hot vomit of a baboon that was in the habit of eating its own feces, if that mixture were then infused with the watery jizzum of a syphilitic pedophile clown.

"Is that not the best thing you ever tasted in your life?" the can asked.

"Hm," I said, feigning an air of indecision as I forced the rancid mush down my gullet. "Now granted, it's pretty good," I lied, "but I don't know that it's the best thing I've ever tasted. I mean, it's hard to say. One TERROR SARDINE is not much food. It's difficult to make an accurate judgment based on such a small sample, ya know?"

If that can of TERROR SARDINES had had a set of ears, anger-smoke would have spewed out of them right about now. The thing trembled with rage before it said, as through clenched teeth, "Okay then, Mr. picky-ass foodie motherfucker. Here's another one."

A second TERROR SARDINE shot out of the can to land in my mouth.

"Man, it's still kinda hard to say," I said after forcing myself to chew and swallow that second putrefied fish and drink more of that revolting sauce. "I mean, these things are good—there's no doubt about that—but these portions are just so small that it's really hard for me to tell if they're the best food I've ever tasted in my life. Sorry, but I really need more to go on. And some more of that TERROR SAUCE too, please."

That gullible, shit-for-brains can tossed me yet another TERROR SARDINE, this one dripping with even more TERROR SAUCE. I pressed on with my ruse, telling the can that I was that much closer to being able to make a final decision with each TERROR SARDINE it tossed in my pie (TERROR SARDINE?) hole. I did this until there was only one TERROR SARDINE left in the can.

See, every can of TERROR SARDINES in TERROR SAUCE is always greater than the sum of its parts: Its sentience and supernatural powers derive from the collective sentience and supernatural powers of each individual TERROR SARDINE and each molecule of TERROR SAUCE packaged in the can. Thus, each time a TERROR SARDINE or a gob of TERROR SAUCE was removed from the can, the larger collective being lost more of its supernatural strength and cunning.

However, this can of TERROR SARDINES managed to figure out my scheme just as its cargo was reduced to one last TERROR SARDINE and one final dollop of TERROR SAUCE.

"Heeeeyy," it said, all slow and stupid now. "A-duhhh. I seeeee whaaaat you're up toooooooo."

"Hey, how about you toss me that last TERROR SARDINE there, big boss. Then I'll know for sure if TERROR SARDINES are the most delicious food on the planet."

"Fuuuucck, yooouuuuuu, motherfuuuuuucker! I'm about to open you up liiiike a caaaaan of motherfuuuuucking sardiiiiiiiiiiiiiiiiiiiiiiiines!"

But the thing was too weak to pry my chest open any more than it already had. It was barely strong enough to keep me pinned down to the floor.

That beret-wearing, violin-playing, slave sardine was in on my plan now. I'd given him a conspiratorial wink at about the eighth or ninth TERROR SARDINE I'd eaten. He'd winked back. Dude was definitely on the level. A second after the can threatened me, the slave sardine stopped playing his music and bashed the last TERROR SARDINE over the head with his violin. The dazed undead fish didn't have a chance to react as the slave sardine then lifted it up in its tiny fins and pitched it out of the can. I caught the slimy little bastard in my left hand and squeezed it into TERROR MUSH.

That last gob of TERROR SAUCE tried to slither away from the sardine violinist, its dozens of remaining eyes darting chaotically around inside its jellied mass in a great panic, but it had nowhere to go. My dude the slave sardine used his violin like a ladle to scoop the gunk up and fling it out of the can. At that moment, the spell of the can of TERROR SARDINES in TERROR SAUCE broke, and my hands were free to unroll my ruined chest like a rug and tuck things back into place to the best of my ability. However, I was now bleeding all over, the broken spell of the can's TERROR MAGIC no longer stopping the flow of my blood as it had done before to prolong my agony during the torture.

"You my dog," I said to the sardine. We gave each other a high five—well, a high one—he slapping my pinkie with one of his pectoral fins. "Listen. I need an ambulance fast or I'm gonna die. My cellie is up on the counter over there. I need you to hop up there and dial 911 for me. Can you do that, my tiny little son?"

"I got your back, bruh," the sardine said. "You saved me from those sick fucks. You freed me from my prison. I'm indebted to you for life."

The sardine did as I asked. He saved my life that day.

By the way, the sardine's name was Fuckin' Francois. Fuckin' Francois and I became besties that day.

In fact, just a week later, we moved in together.

***

"Yo, I got your back," Fuckin' Francois said to me one morning five years later. I was sitting at my little kitchen table enjoying a breakfast of Lucky Charms. Fuckin' Francois stood upright on the opposite end of the table, propped up on the forked prongs of his tail fin like feet, red beret in place on his head, and diminutive violin slung over his dorsal fin with a strap like a guitar.

"I know you do, man," I said after shoveling a heaping spoonful of soggy Lucky Charms into my Lucky Charms hole. "You don't need to tell me that."

"No, man. I mean, I *really* got your back."

"I know you do, dude. We've been friends for five years now. During that time, you've gotten me out of more than a few scrapes. Shit, we've traveled the goddamn world three times over, you and I. We've saved each other's asses dozens of times and robbed like over a hundred banks together. We've banged more hot women and hot female sardines than I can count. I got your back too, Fuckin' Francois. We're a team. Bros for life, homeboy!"

"No, you still don't quite understand. See, I *actually* have your back."

"Like I said, Fuckin' Francois, I know you do," I replied, my voice now edged with just a hint of annoyance. "I got yours too!"

"Dude! I'm trying to tell you that I *literally* have your back!"

I chuckled. "Now you're just talkin' silly. You high or something? Hey, if you're holding out on me with some diggity-dank bubonic chronic or somethin', Imma be reeeaaaal pissed, dolla."

Fuckin' Francois turned away from me, leaned down towards the chair behind him, a chair that I thought was empty. Now I could see a black garbage bag propped up on the seat. I watched curiously as Fuckin' Francois jumped onto the bag, loosened the red drawstring, and reached inside with his little fins to haul something out. (Bear in mind that Fuckin' Francois was strong as hell for a normal non-TERROR sardine.)

My expression of curiosity morphed into one of abject horror when Fuckin' Francois extracted a long, wide, bloody slab of meat from the bag: a sheet of raw flesh sheathed on one side in a layer of nearly hairless, pale skin dotted here and there with a few familiar-looking moles. He let the unskinned hunk of meat drop onto the tabletop with a sick, wet thud.

"See?" the tiny fish asked.

The awful realization finally setting in, I set my spoon down and slowly brought my hands behind me to feel my back. Where my probing fingertips should have encountered smooth skin stretched tautly over sculpted muscle and bone, they instead touched the slick, wet bones of my exposed ribcage. My fingers then traced a path along the slimy ridges of my exposed spinal column before encountering the sickly soft, curved shapes of my kidneys followed by the moist, fibrous texture of the expanding and contracting sacs that were my lungs.

"This morning while you were sleeping," the sardine said matter-of-factly, "I soaked a rag with chloroform and put it over your face to keep you from gaining consciousness while I prepped you. Then I injected your back with a strong local anesthetic and administered an epidural block. That's why you're not in any pain right now. However, I didn't do anything to suppress the bleeding. So I'm guessing you have maybe twenty seconds or so to live, brah."

I glanced down at the pool of my lifeblood blooming on the floor, suddenly feeling cold and faint.

"Yo, I thought you were...my...my boy," I croaked. That's when the sardine jumped down to the floor, careful to avoid my blood, and hopped over to the other side of the kitchen, where, to my great surprise, I saw my mom standing in the doorway. She held a suitcase in each hand: one was quite large, while the other was about the size of a 9-volt battery. The little one I knew belonged to Fuckin' Francois.

"Mom? Not...not you too?"

"I'm afraid so, Tommy," she said. "Fuckin' Francois and I have been, well, fuckin' for about two months now. He and I are taking all the money you two earned robbing banks and moving to Bora Bora. Sorry, honey. Granted, a mother's unconditional love for her child is one of the most powerful and enduring things in the universe. But that love just doesn't hold a candle to the exquisite pleasure of having a handsome-ass, smooth-talkin', beret-wearin', crack pipe-smokin' sardine burrow deep into your colon to play Pagapepperoni on his pointy, but well-lubricated fiddle."

"It's Paganini, not Pagapepperoni, you stupid, white-trash bitch!" Fuckin' Francois said as he leaped up from the floor and slapped my mom hard across the face, causing her to giggle and blush. "And it's a *violin*, not a fiddle, you ignorant, Jabba the Hutt-lookin', crackwhore!" he said as he sprung up into the air a second time to slap Mom across the other side of her face, making her giggle and blush even more.

"Hey, you keep you dirty hands—I mean fins—off my mom! And you can't talk to her like that! Man, fuck you, Fuckin' Francois! And fuck that cheap hipster beret of yours. I'll...fuckin'...squash...you...to..." were my last words.

I slipped out of my chair, fell hard onto the bloody floor, died, and was reincarnated as a goddamn miserable speck of TERROR ALGAE floating on the slimy surface of a TERROR LAKE, only to be gobbled up by a TERROR SARDINE three seconds after my reincarnation.

After that second death, I didn't reincarnate into anything else.

That was fuckin' it.

***

MORAL OF THE STORY:

Don't trust anyone. Ever. Yeah, not even your own mom. Because the second you think someone has your back, you just might find out that they ACTUALLY HAVE YOUR BACK!!!!!!!!!!!!!!!!!!!!!!!!!!!!!

Not That It Matters, but the War of 1812 Was Kinda Hawt

After logging into his computer and taking a few sips of coffee, Brian began his workday the way he always did: by closing his eyes and pressing his thumbs against his eyelids with the intent to kill himself by driving his thumbs back into the frontal lobes of his brain. But as usual, he failed to muster up enough nerve to go through with it. Instead, he pressed his eyeballs only hard enough to cause some grainy blobs of color to swirl behind his eyelids. As usual, as soon as he felt the first pang of real pain, he wimped out and let up on the pressure.

It wasn't that Brian was depressed. He did not hate his job. He was not lonely. Neither was he seriously ill nor was he beset by any serious legal or financial troubles. Rather, Brian's problem was shame. It was embarrassment. It was self-disgust.

It was complete mortification.

Damn, what the hell was I thinking? he thought for possibly the ten-thousandth time.

Brian was referring to several years ago when he and his frat buddies had been really into that short-lived swing revival of the late 1900s and early 2000s, when bands like Big Bad Voodoo Daddy, Squirrel Nut Zippers, and Cherry Poppin' Daddies had enjoyed their little moment. Without exercising the slightest degree of scrutiny or discretion, Brian had eaten that swing stuff right up. He'd bought all the CDs, gone to all the shows, and taken dance lessons to learn all the swing moves. He'd even worn a zoot suit. Sure, many years had passed since Brian had last attended a swing show or donned a zoot suit, but there were certain acknowledged wellsprings of embarrassment, certain unpardonable follies of youth, from which one could never hope to recover.

Being really into that swing revival of the late 1900s and early 2000s was one such folly.

Christ, I even wore a fucking zoot suit, Brian thought for the ten-thousandth time, shaking his head as he continued to press his thumbnails into his shut eyelids, now applying pressure again.

"Nice haircut," Meredith said, startling him.

Brian let his thumbs drop from his eyes as he swiveled around to face his coworker, presenting her with a baby-smooth mug that hung beneath his newly acquired, close-cropped crew cut.

"And he shaved too!" Meredith gasped. Just yesterday, Brian had sported an unironic lumberjack beard and a head of long, dark hair that had fallen past the middle of his back.

"Yeah, with summer almost here," Brian said, "I figured it was a good time for me to lose the mountain man look."

"Glad ya did. I nearly forgot there was a handsome guy hiding underneath there," Meredith said good-naturedly, perhaps even flirtatiously, though it was hard to tell with her.

Brian blushed a little regardless.

Meredith eyed the vintage *Dukes of Hazzard* lunchbox sitting next to the computer monitor on Brian's desk. The metal lunchbox was standard in its rectangular dimensions, measuring 8.5 inches in length and 6.75 inches in width. However, where most lunchboxes were about three to four inches in height, Brian's was nearly a foot high.

"So you took care of your beard and your Samson mane, but what about that lunchbox?" Meredith asked, pointing. "Are you going to get that trimmed too?"

"Eventually. I was thinking I'd let it grow out a little while longer. I've never done that before."

"You do know it's not currently fashionable to let your lunchbox grow long, right?" The young woman's sassy tone was tinged with a note of ridicule.

Brian chuckled before he lied. "Since when do I care about what's fashionable, Meredith?"

Meredith wrinkled her nose in disapproval before sashaying away.

***

Not that it matters, but Meredith was kinda hawt.

***

Brian continued to let his lunchbox grow. Every so often, simply out of force of habit, he found himself tempted to take it to the barber and have it trimmed down to a nice, respectable, standard height of four inches or so. But he resisted the temptation, even when, in mid-July, Best Cuts emailed him a coupon for four dollars off any adult or child haircut *or* five dollars off a lunchbox cut.

Brian liked his long *Dukes of Hazzard* lunchbox, trends and fashions be damned.

Right about when his lunchbox reached a height of five feet, it started to grow at a curve, not unlike human fingernails do. As summer wore on, the lunchbox began to follow an increasingly meandering growth pattern, twisting, turning, and looping like Play-Doh forced through a plastic extruder. By the end of August, the chaotically curving container measured forty feet across from its farthest points. It no longer fit through the front door at the cubicle farm where Brian worked. As such, his employer was obligated to knock out part of the front wall of the building and install a large cargo door to accommodate the lunchbox. It was either that or have Brian sue the company for discriminating against him and his lunchbox.

Obviously, standing the lunchbox upright on its base was no longer possible. Instead, Brian had to lay it on its side on the floor. As a consequence, the lunchbox filled the entire cubicle row where his workstation was located. Anyone needing to walk down that row had to step over and duck under the sundry, asymmetrical twists and bends of the lunchbox. Fresh out of college, a particularly unlucky new hire tripped over the thing on her first day of work, cracking her skull open on the floor, and dying in the ambulance en route to the hospital.

***

Not that it matters, but Brian was kinda hawt too.

***

Brian worked for Training-Tech Corporation (NDAQ: TR-TEC). The company's sole business activity was to create and update training software designed to instruct new employees at Training-Tech on how to generate and update training software used to teach new trainees at Training-Tech how to produce and modify training software aimed at educating recent Training-Tech hirees in the proper methods by which they were required to design and update training software for the internal purpose of instructing new Training-Tech employees on how to generate and upgrade training software engineered to indoctrinate recent Training-Tech recruits in the established procedures by which new members of the Training-Tech team learned how to properly create and improve the training software required to inculcate untrained Training-Tech employees in the long-practiced methodologies by which uninitiated Training-Tech staffers were required to learn how to generate *new* and improve upon *existing* training software expressly for the purpose of informing new Training-Tech personnel on how to beget and update training software designed for the ad hoc function of educating Training-Tech hirelings in how to properly...

***

Not that it matters, but the girl who died from tripping over Brian's lunchbox was kinda hawt too.

***

Tim Cruthers, Brian's supervisor, stopped by one morning to talk. The balding, middle-aged, middle manager banged his forehead on a high, twisting arc of lunchbox as he ducked into Brian's cube. "Ouch, goddamnit!"

Brian, who had been engaged in another unsuccessful attempt to drive his thumbs back into his brain, let his hands drop to his sides as he spun around to face the man.

"Oh, hi, Tim."

"Hi, Brian," Tim said, rubbing his forehead. "Listen. We need to talk about your lunchbox. There have been complaints."

Brian's brow furrowed as he grimaced. "Tim, I have every right to let my lunchbox grow long. That new girl who died, I feel really bad for her and her family—I do—but she should've been watching where the fuck she was going."

"You're allowed to keep your lunchbox long. That's not why I stopped by. The problem is the picture on the lid. See, many people are offended by the Confederate flag on the roof of the *Dukes of Hazzard* car, so I'm afraid I'm gonna have to ask you to cover up that flag or else get a new lid for the lunchbox."

Eyes rolling, Brian sighed. "Alright, I'll take care of it."

"Thanks, Bri. Good talk." As Tim turned to dip out of Brian's cube, he banged his head on the lunchbox again. "Ouch, goddamnit!"

***

Not that it matters, but Tim was kinda hawt too.

***

Later that afternoon, Best Cuts emailed Brian a coupon for four dollars off any adult or child haircut *or* five dollars off a lunchbox cut *or* two dollars off a lunchbox replacement lid. At quitting time, Brian printed out the coupon, logged out of his computer, and dragged his lunchbox out through the cargo door into the parking lot, where he tied it to the bumper of his 1993 Honda Disaccord.

At Best Cuts, Brian handed the coupon to the employee standing behind the counter. The employee's name was the War of 1812. The reason the employee's name was the War of 1812 was because the employee *was* the War of 1812. Somehow, due to forces far beyond anyone's understanding, the War of 1812 had been yanked out of history and materialized into this sentient, human-like being who presently worked at Best Cuts to put bread on the table and beer in the fridge. At a glance, the War of 1812 resembled the faceless ghost of an obese man—smoky in texture, gray in color, but unmistakably anthropomorphic in form, having a large, round torso, a pair of arms, a pair of legs, and a neckless head. Anyone who peered into the War of 1812's vaporous torso long enough might be treated to a dramatic glimpse of a land battle fought along the American-Canadian frontier between the United States and Britain's native American allies, or perhaps even a thrilling naval skirmish on the Great Lakes.

"I'd like a replacement lid for my lunchbox," Brian said to the War of 1812.

"Which replacement lid do you want?" the war asked, its voice a low-pitched frog croak.

"What do you have?"

"*Freddy vs. Jason*, *Alien vs. Predator*, and *Mr. Furley vs. Mr. Roper.*"

Brian thought about it for a moment before saying, "*Freddy vs. Jason.*"

After the War of 1812 reached beneath the register to grab a *Freddy vs. Jason* lunchbox lid, it asked, "Where's your lunchbox?"

"Out in the parking lot. It's kind of long."

Carrying the *Freddy vs. Jason* lunchbox lid in one blurry hand, the War of 1812 waddled out from behind the counter. Brian followed it out into the front parking lot, where the war paused alongside the sprawling structure that was Brian's lunchbox.

"It *is* gettin' kinda of long," the War of 1812 said, sounding slightly concerned. "You sure you don't want me to give it a cut too?"

"I like it this way. I just need the lid replaced."

The War of 1812 nodded, shrugged, and began circling the lunchbox, searching for the lid. When the war found it, it asked, "So how do you stop your lunch from falling deep down inside here?"

"I duct tape my food and my thermos to the inside wall just beneath the lid."

"Ah, good thinking." The War of 1812 then struggled to kneel down on the pavement, as if its ethereal form were hindered by old, achy joints and bones contained within it. And perhaps that was the case. The war used a small screwdriver to unfasten the two hinge assemblies affixing the offensive lid to the lunchbox.

"Now what in Samhain is that?" the war said after it removed the lid. It leaned its featureless lump of a head close to the opening of the rectangular tunnel.

"What is what?" Brian asked.

"Come down here and listen, son."

Brian knelt down beside the War of 1812, positioned his ear near the opening of the lunchbox. He did hear something: a low, steady rumbling. Faint, but growing louder. He scowled, perplexed. "It almost sounds like...like there's a car in there."

"Yep. My thought exactly."

Brian placed the palm of his hand on the side of the lunchbox—the metal vibrated. The rumbling grew louder, its vibration intensifying into a visible shake as something sped through the lunchbox's snaky coils, something evidently headed for the light at the end of the tunnel. Brian and the War of 1812 backed away from the opening to be safe.

When the General Lee—the iconic car from *The Dukes of Hazzard*—flew out of the lunchbox moments later, for a split second, it was the size of a remote-controlled toy before it expanded to actual car size. To the astonishment of both Brian and the War of 1812, the orange, Confederate flag-emblazoned, 1969 Dodge Charger landed a hundred feet away on the other side of the parking lot in a spinning, screeching, 180-degree stunt turn before it zoomed back across the lot to halt alongside the lunchbox in a second tire-smoking stop.

Jason was at the wheel. Jason, as in Jason Voorhees.

Freddy Krueger rode shotgun.

Alien and Predator were in the backseat.

"Round and Round" by Ratt blasted from the vehicle's front speakers. At the same time, NWA's "Fuck tha Police" cranked from the car's back speakers. But rather than create a jumbled cacophony, the simultaneous playing of the two songs was oddly synchronized so they could be enjoyed concurrently without disrupting each other.

Jason revved the General Lee's souped-up engine as Freddy dangled his arm out the passenger window, idly undulating and fanning his metal claws. Freddy said, "Hey, we're gonna go pick up Mr. Furley, Mr. Roper, Douglas Hackle, Tupac, Snoop, and [*insert your name here, dear reader*], and then go hit the bars. You guys wanna come?"

Taken aback, Brian gulped, said, "Um, no thank you."

"Aw, hells yeah!" the War of 1812 croaked as it lumbered to the side of the Charger.

Alien reached from the backseat with its long, powerful, sinewy arms, pulled the War of 1812 in through the passenger window, plopped it down in the middle between it and Predator.

"Sure you don't wanna come with us, kid?" Freddy asked. "It promises to be a grand ol' time."

"No thanks. I really should be getting back to the office to do more work," Brian lied.

"Aw, c'mon. You may never get another opportunity like this in your lifetime."

"I'd like to come along. Really I would. It's just that...that..."

"It's just that what?"

"It's just that I'm not that cool. I'm not cool enough to hang out with you guys."

"Nonsense!" Freddy said. "I mean, look who just got into the car with us: the War of 1812 for chrissakes! I mean, you can't get much more uncool than the War of 1812, right? At a glance, son, you seem alright to me. And I'm usually a pretty good judge of character. And if you were uncool at some point in the past, who gives a shit? The present is all that matters. We can forgive and forget the missteps of our past, no?"

"Um, I'm afraid not everything can be forgiven and forgotten, Freddy," Brian said, averting his eyes and dropping his head in shame.

"Whaddya do, kid?"

"Remember that short-lived swing revival that happened in the late 1900s and early 2000s?"

"Yeah, unfortunately."

"Well, I was…into it. I was *really* into it. I was a swing-bro, Freddy. I bought all the CDs, went to all the shows. I even took swing dance lessons. I even wore a a "

"A zoot suit?" Freddy finished for him, his hoarse voice conveying a mixture of disgust and incredulity.

"Yeah," Brain mumbled, dropping his head even lower.

"WHAT?!?" Jason asked in utter astonishment. "You were into that 90's swing shit? Like, for real?" It was the first time he had spoken to *anyone* about *anything* since drowning in Crystal Lake when he was a boy.

"Yeah, I was."

"Wow," Freddy said. "I guess I'm not such a good judge of character after all. I'd eviscerate you right now myself, put you out of your goddamn misery, except we're running late. Jason, let's bounce, baby!"

Jason threw the car into drive, peeled out, and ran over Brian's lunchbox, destroying it.

***

Standing in the Best Cuts parking lot before the mangled wreckage of his lunchbox, Brian balled his hands into fists, flipped his thumbs up, and raised them to his closed eyelids. Determined to succeed this time, he pressed his thumbs into his eyeballs harder than he'd ever pressed them before.

Harder.
And harder still.
And finally...
POP!!!!!!!!!!!!!!!!!

***

Not that it matters, but the War of 1812 was kinda hawt too.

The Unpursued Person

The historic South Side Market had always been one of the most charming, beloved landmarks of Dapperdog, Ohio, a place where typically more than a hundred fifty vendors gathered every day to hawk their wares—meats, seafood, produce, ethnic foods, baked goods, spices, flowers, etc.—to customers from near and afar. Back when I taught at Dapperdog University, I was lucky enough to rent rooms only three blocks west of "The Market," as it was known. Late in the morning on most Sundays, if the weather were pleasant, I was wont to enjoy a leisurely stroll there, particularly if I were running low on fair trade organic coffee beans or artisanal pickled beets.

The last time I visited The Market was one such Sunday morning during spring break, circa the late 90s. Being on vacation, I had a little extra spring in my step that day. A pleasant breeze seemed to propel me along the sidewalk as I briskly walked those three blocks. Upon my arrival, I browsed the stalls of The Market's outdoor produce arcade for a few minutes before making my way into the interior concourse of the main building—an immense and cavernous neo-Byzantine brick structure that boasted a high vaulted ceiling and a lofty clock tower. I immediately visited my favorite seller of artisanal pickled foods and purchased a jumbo jar of beets.

Ah, the delightful smells, sights, and sounds of that big, old place!

I must admit that, as an avid people watcher, I probably patronized The Market as much for its people as I did its goods. But of more interest to me than the actual customers and vendors in The Market were those individuals who *pursued* the customers and vendors. Granted, there was nothing unusual about this type of public stalking, as it were, and in this respect, The Market was like any other public place in the world. For it is common knowledge that whenever *anyone* leaves the comfort of their home to venture out into public *for any reason whatsoever*, within moments of walking out their door, they are pursued by some stranger. Again, this was a normal and highly mundane phenomenon, a thing hardly ever discussed by anyone. However, I had always been somewhat fascinated by it.

Take, for example, the surly-looking elderly gentleman I saw that morning hovering over the sausage table, evidently deliberating on whether to buy the bratwurst or the knockwurst. Though I didn't notice this man's pursuer immediately, it didn't take long for me to find him: After a moment's searching, I espied a long-bearded, hollow-cheeked face hovering in the shadows beneath a table three stalls down, the hidden individual's hawk-like gaze fixed firmly on this old man.

And that mother I noticed pushing a baby stroller a few aisles over. As the young woman inspected the sundry cheeses stacked on the table before her, not twenty feet away, a man in a trench coat, his face mostly hidden by a forward-tilted fedora, watched her from over the top of the newspaper he was pretending to read. Not far down the same aisle in the opposite direction, a small, pale, waxy face wearing a crow beak masquerade mask peeked out from the darkness between two crates, this visage's white, nearly glowing eyes trained on the infant sleeping in said mother's stroller.

    Searching for these pursuers had always been a favorite diversion of mine, a game even. They were everywhere, these beings—these pursuers or stalkers or trackers or followers or shadows or whatever you wished to call them—some standing in plain sight like Mr. Trench Coat, others half-hidden, others nearly invisible, no more than the wet glimmer of an eye staring up through a grate in the floor. It had always given me a sort of strange sense of peace knowing that everyone in the world, without exception, whenever they ventured out into the public, was pursued in this way, almost as if these pursuers were guardian angels. Of course, these pursuers were anything but guardian angels and, truth be told, had much more in common with devils than angels. Still, any given individual's pursuer was perfectly harmless so long as the pursued person succeeded in ignoring the pursuer's presence.

    So why not then imagine them as guardian angels?

***

    I noticed him shortly after I spotted the pursuers of the mother and her baby. A white man of medium build and height like myself, he was buying spinach gnocchi and a jar of tomato basil sauce. Late thirties or early forties, casually dressed, brow-line glasses, receding hairline, and the start of a beer gut. Like me, he was neither handsome nor homely, but somewhere in between. In fact, this individual would have been wholly unremarkable had he not lacked a pursuer.

Yes, as incredible as it sounds, and though I searched all the way up and down the aisle ten times over, I could not locate this man's pursuer. As such, I had to assume the man's very well-hidden chaser would reveal himself or herself just as soon as the shopper resumed walking. But this did not happen. After making his purchase, the man drifted through the labyrinthine aisles of The Market for another fifteen minutes or so, his only other purchase that day being a bottle of wine he picked up just before he left. I tailed him the entire time. To my dismay, I was able to match up each and every person I passed with their respective and never-too-far-off pursuers.

But not this man.

Needless to say, I grew more and more frustrated the longer I followed him, my frustration giving way to a terrible uneasiness by the time he exited The Market. I followed him through the main doors of the building, certain I'd spot the man's pursuer in the city streets—perhaps another trench coat guy hiding behind a newspaper, a half-visible face peeking around the corner of a building or out from a shadowy alley, a crouched, silhouetted form moving stealthily along the rooftops.

But no.

Nothing.

Oh, there were plenty of pursuers out there, alright, just none in pursuit of this particular person: this unpursued person.

Well, except me, of course. But I didn't count.

At least not yet.

After following him through the city for another ten minutes, I thought: *So what am I to do now?* Turn away and walk home in the opposite direction? Pretend I never saw this man? Was I to live the rest of my life denying his existence to myself—this unthinkable anomaly, this affront to the natural order of the universe, this unpursued, impossible man?

I was left with little choice, really: I resolved then and there to become the man's pursuer myself. Which I suppose was apropos, considering I already had a head start on the business.

Moments after I made my decision, the man paused in front of the entrance to an apartment building. With his back to me, he began to slowly turn his head to look over his shoulder.

He knows he's being followed! I thought as I quickly ducked behind a shrub. Now, granted, I was no expert in these matters—I'm not sure that anyone was—but I knew that one should avoid being aware of one's own pursuer, at least as much as was possible. Sure, in an academic sense, we all knew our pursuers were out there in the world, never lurking too far off. But as far as day to day living went, most people were about as cognizant of their pursuers as they were of their own respiration or the beating of their hearts. And the less aware of them you were, the less likely it was they would ever *get you*; for it was common knowledge that the only individuals who were ever caught and killed by their pursuers were those mentally unstable souls who constantly thought about their pursuers, and who, as a result, at some point either consciously fled them or else tried to find, confront, and fight them.

You better be reeeeaaal careful, homeboy, I thought as I watched the man through a tiny opening in the shrub. After looking over his shoulder and not spotting me, he turned away and resumed walking at a faster pace. I continued to follow him as he headed southwest toward the edge of town. Along the way, every few minutes he stopped to glance nervously over his shoulder to see if anyone was tailing him, prompting me to duck out of sight behind more shrubs, mailboxes, building corners, and other pedestrians.

I wanted to shout at him, "You're not supposed to do that! Stop looking for me! Just ignore me already!" but etiquette strictly forbade such interaction: Everyone knew that, with the exception of a pursuit coming to violent end, pursuers never spoke to the pursued and vice versa. But the man refused to stop looking over his shoulder in search of me, even as he passed through the last neighborhood of old houses that marked the edge of Dapperdog proper, at which point he pushed onward into the hilly, rural purlieu that lay beyond the city limits.

We found ourselves on a country road, me trailing him at a steady, inconspicuous distance of about a hundred feet, the city shrinking behind us. To avoid being seen, I stayed just inside the edge of the dense woods that flanked the road. By this point, the man was glancing over his shoulder every ten seconds or so, and his accelerating stride was almost a full-on jog.

Don't do it, I thought, when he finally let his bag of groceries drop to the ground.

But he did it: The man took off in a sprint, fleeing me.

You dumbass, I thought.

Unfortunately, a pursuer had to do what a pursuer had to do. I was obliged to give chase.

The man cut into the woods, hoping to shake me. I charged down after him into a shallow gorge, where the chase took us along the path of a dry streambed, me steadily closing in on my quarry. Before long, the man tripped over a rock, twisting his ankle and hitting the ground hard.

Lying on his back and facing me as I slowed my pace and caught my breath, the man held up his trembling palms in a gesture of surrender and an entreaty for mercy. Just beyond his head and blocking any further progress along the gorge was a large, twisted deadfall like a beaver's dam.

He was trapped.

As I mentioned before, the exact methods, devices, codes, customs, and rules of pursuers had always been for the most part hidden from us normie non-pursuer folk. However, a newfound, primitive instinct rose within me at this moment—the pursuer's instinct—effectively making up for what I lacked in practical knowledge about the business.

I set down my jar of artisanal pickled beets, threw up my arms above my head, hooked my hands into claws, and took up a lumbering Frankenstein gait as I continued to approach him. "I'm the monster now!" I said as I twisted my face into a wrathful grimace and roared like some terrible beast: "Rarrrrrrrrrrrrrrrrrrrh!"

"Oh, G-G-God, no! Please don't fucking kill me!" Tears welled in the man's terrified eyes.

"Rarrrrrrrrrrrrrrrrrrrrrrrrh!" I was mere feet away from him now.

"Oh, shit. Oh, shit. Oh, shit. Please! I…I don't wanna die!" The man was sobbing now. And I couldn't quite tell you why at the time, but something about his weeping was not commensurate with the situation. Granted, he was about to die, so the man had every right to bawl his eyes out while pleading for his life. But his ridiculously loud sobs were tinged with something other than fear, horror, and disbelief. I just couldn't put my finger on what that thing was exactly.

Eh, not my problem, I thought, hardening myself to the unpleasant task at hand, a task I had never asked for but one I was obligated to finish. I continued roaring, closing in on him slowly and tortuously: "Rarrrrrrrrrrrrrrrrrrrrrrrrrh!"

"Oh, just get it over with already, will ya? I fuckin' deserve to die. I'm such a loser!" The man burst into more heavy sobs as he began to punch himself hard in the face. That's when I realized what other qualities infused his awful, nearly unendurable blubbering.

Shame. Shame and deep regret.

Though I continued hovering above him with my claw-curled hands raised aggressively in striking position, I stopped inching forward and said, "What's your goddamn problem, hoss?"

"I've…I've pretty much wasted my entire life. And here I am about to fucking die!"

"Whaddaya mean you wasted your entire life?"

"Aw, you wouldn't understand."

"Oh, no? Try me. If anything, it will extend your miserable life a little bit longer, asshole. Lemme guess: You regret not starting a family of your own?"

"Oh, no. Nothing like that. I have a beautiful wife and three healthy kids at home."

"Lemme try again. Despite your wonderful little family, you're unhappy in your chosen career. You regret partying your youth away, and you wish you would've gone to college to become a lawyer or doctor or architect or something, right?"

"Oh, no. That's not my problem either. I'm actually a founding senior partner of a very successful architectural firm. And I love my work, too."

"Okay, I give up then. What's your goddamn problem?"

"Alright, I'll tell you. My problem is that…that…"

"Go ahead. Spit it out already, slice!"

"Okay, Okay! Here goes: My problem is that…that right now, as we speak, there are horses out there in the world that have tagged more cute white chicks than I have."

As soon as he uttered this confession he burst into a fresh batch of baby sobs. *Waaaaaaaaaaa….!*

I was silent for a spell. When his crying started to abate, the man peered up at my face. Seemed he interpreted my silence as indicating ignorance of what he was talking about.

"Maybe I should explain," he said. "See, on the internet—well, on the dark underbelly of the internet, specifically—there are certain websites that feature—"

"I know what the hell you're talking about, dickhead. You think you're the only person who's ever seen fucked up shit on the internet before?"

"Well, okay, you know then. Yeah, I just can't friggin' believe that there are horses out there that have nailed more cute white chicks than—"

"FUCK YOU!" I spit-screamed at him. "What the hell do you think *I* am, huh, pal? Some sort of Casanova or rock star or something?"

"I'm sorry. I was just talking about me. I certainly meant no offense to you, really. I—"

"You think *you've* struggled with the ladies? Well listen to this, fuckface. Every time I take out a woman on a date, I bring along a jumbo jar of artisanal pickled beets with me. See, there's no point in me ever looking at a menu when I go to a restaurant. During a dinner or lunch date, when I inevitably ask the waiter for an empty plate and then dump a heaping mound of artisanal pickled beets onto it, I'm obliged to explain to my date that artisanal pickled beets are the only food I eat. Breakfast, lunch, dinner, and snacks. Not because I particularly like artisanal pickled beets. Because I don't. But they're the only food in the world that doesn't make me fucking puke.

"So, let me ask you, Mr. Boohoo-There-Are-Horses-Out-There-That-Have-Nailed-More-Cute-White-Chicks-Than-I-Have: How many second dates do you think I've ever managed to get, eh? Go ahead and make your best guess."

"Um, like, zero maybe?" the teary-eyed man said.

"YOU'RE GODDAMN RIGHT ZERO! And here you are crying about how you're the only dude in the world who's bagged less attractive white girls than most porn-horses have, you self-absorbed, egocentric, little prick!" I spun about-face, crouched down to unscrew the lid of my jar of artisanal pickled beets, reached in, and grabbed a handful.

"Now choke on these, you smug, self-pitying bastard!" I said as I mashed the juicy, red, disgusting things into his face. Like a picky-eating toddler, he refused to open his mouth, so I pinched his nose shut with my free hand. When his lips finally parted so he could take a breath, I rammed the beets home, force-feeding him another two handfuls so that his cheeks were to the point of bursting.

Ignoring my new pursuer instinct, I changed my mind about killing the man.

I now had a far more fitting end in mind for this asshole.

In analytic geometry, there's something called an asymptote; simply put, an asymptote is a straight line approached by a curved line where the two lines never meet, getting closer and closer as they approach infinity. This mathematical function was analogous to what I planned to do to this jerkoff: Starting at a distance of only a few feet away, I would resume my pursuit of the man, but I would move toward him *very, very slowly*, ever closing the distance between us but never actually reaching him.

I would pursue this motherfucker infinitely.

To make my appearance more horrifying for this purpose, I plucked my own two eyes out of their sockets, ate them, and replaced them with two artisanal pickled beets. I then resumed my position, threw my arms up, hooked my hands into claws, and roared like a beast, edging toward my blubbering, groveling quarry until the end of fucking time.

***

Eternity's a long time. As such, I like to break up the monotony of my unending task by alternating between roaring like a beast and shouting the word, "CREEEEEEEEE-CRAWWWWWWWWWWW!!!"

At some point during the eons, one of the remaining artisanal pickled beets in the jar grew bored out of its little fucking skull, hopped out onto the ground, grabbed two twigs, and started tapping out drumbeats on the side of the jar.

I must say, that little beet could drop some sick beats.

I Won the MegaSuperLotto

A few weeks ago, I won the MegaSuperLotto.

The jackpot was $932 million. I had the only winning ticket. It was the largest lottery payout to a single individual in the history of lotteries.

A few nights prior to purchasing my ticket, the winning numbers—1, 20, 34, 72, 84, 94, 98—were revealed to me in an über-fucked up nightmare in which I had doggy-style sex with my sister at a Motel 6 in Detroit.

Okay, I'll come clean: The nightmare was a tad more disturbing and complicated than that. In it, my big sis had my dad's head, my mom's arms, my grandpap's legs, and my baby brother's kidneys (I could not see the kidneys, of course, but as I was the semi-omniscient host of this nightmare, I was privy to that knowledge). And if all that wasn't fucked-up enough, my dad's head was screwed on backwards, so that his face glowered back at me with big, wet eyes of glaring condemnation throughout the entirety of the perverse sex act. As I subjected the Dad-headed, hybrid family-thing to my ungentle thrusts, I was repulsed—nay, sickened to the very core of my being. I longed to pull myself off the monstrosity, to run as far away from that motel room as my dream-legs would carry me.

But at the same time, part of me did not want to pull away.

And that was perhaps the scariest thing of all.

Then, just before I climaxed, the Dad-head croaked those seven winning lottery numbers to me in the raspy, throat-cancer voice of my grandma, and I awoke with a start.

Anyhow, I didn't know it at the time, but the federal tax rate on lottery earnings in the U.S. was 347.46%. That meant I owed Uncle Sam a staggering and completely unpayable $323.8 billion! And I also didn't know it at the time, but a recent amendment to the U.S. Constitution stated that a lottery winner's refusal or inability to pay the federal taxes on his or her lottery earnings was punishable by death by firing squad.

***

When they executed me, one of the dozens of copper-jacketed .30-30 rounds that tore through me just so happened to penetrate my skull and strike my basal ganglia—a bundle of neurons situated near the center of the brain. In addition to other neural functions, the basal ganglia is involved with the perception of the passage of time. I died more or less instantly; however, due to the specific shape, velocity, temperature, and direction of the bullet that obliterated my basal ganglia, my subjective perception of time was vastly distorted in that final instant so that the moment of my death stretched out like a wad of chewing gum. To be specific, from my point of view, it took me approximately 378 years to die. Now had that same bullet hit my basal ganglia just a nanometer to the left or a micrometer to the right, or had the bullet entered my skull at a speed that was a few millimeters per second slower than the speed it actually did enter, I might have experienced a more or less normal, instant sort of death. Then again, perhaps my death would have been protracted even longer. Who the hell knows? The human brain is infinitely full of quirks.

Anyway, point being my death sucked. Big time.

Now I'm a ghost. And upon further reflection, considering I'm a ghost and have left all worldly affairs permanently behind, I might as well come clean—for real this time.

Here goes: Remember that nightmare I said I had? Well, it wasn't a nightmare.

Not only is that Dad-headed sister thing real, it's my next of kin. Which means not only did the thing inherit my MegaSuperLotto winnings when I died, but it also inherited the tax burden on those earnings.

As a consequence, the Dad-headed sister thing is scheduled for execution by firing squad tomorrow morning.

***

I wonder if we'll find each other here on the dark, misty-purple plane of the spirit world. If we do meet again, I wonder if our incorporeal, quasi-ectoplasmic forms will be able to engage in sex. Of course it goes without saying that the very notion of such an unspeakable, depraved reunion repulses me, sickens me to the very core of my spectral being.

But still I wonder.

Okay, I'll come clean again: Part of me does want that unspeakable, depraved reunion to take place.

And that's what scares me.

Okay, okay, alright, alright, I'll come *completely* clean this time: My desire for that unspeakable, depraved reunion doesn't scare me at all actually.

That's because I want to fuck the shit out of that fucking thing again.
That thing is fucking hawt!!!!!!!!!!!!!!!!!!!!!!!!!

A Small Owl with a Broken Wing (from Compton)

A small owl with a broken wing (from Compton) trudged down a country road in Nebraska until it came to a stop in front of a run-down farmhouse set back about a stone's throw from the road and surrounded by acres of waist-high hay. An old man sat in a rocking chair on the front porch, one gnarled hand gripping a 16-ounce can of PBR in his lap.

After the owl and old man regarded one another for a stretch, the owl toddled up the gravel drive, came to a halt at the bottom of the sunken steps leading up to the wraparound porch. The little bird tilted its head back to look up at the old man.

"Imma for-real-ass motherfuckin' gangsta," it squeaked. "Betta ask somebody." It attempted to throw a gang sign with its good wing, but failed.

"Speak up, son. I don't hear so well these days."

"Imma for-real-ass motherfuckin' gangsta," the owl said louder. "Betta ask somebody."

"A for-real-ass what?" the old man asked, reaching to adjust the volume on his hearing aid.

"A FOR-REAL-ASS GANGSTA!"

"I said speak up, not shout, son!" The old man frowned. "So yer a gangster, eh? You mean like Al Capone or Lucky Luciano?"

"Who dey? And it's pronounced gangSTA, not gangSTER. Imma legit-ass gangsta straight outta Compton. Imma a rappa too."

"Compton? Never heard of it. Is that north of the crick?"

"It's in Southern Cali, yo."

"California! What the hell ya doin' here in 'braska, son?"

"Me and mah squad was at this bomb-ass, whizz-bang houseparty in East Compton, yo, when these foos rolled up on us, did a drive by. So me and mah squad, we ran outside, got into a gunfight with these punk-ass suckas. I rekt a couple of dem little-dicked bitches with my nine, but I also took a cap in mah wing. We all went running in different directions right before the po-po got there. I was losing blood, gettin' all delirious, seeing devils and demons n' shit, but I just kept runnin', yo. Now here I am, stuck with your old, droopy-lookin' white ass."

"Not sure I understood everythin' ya just said, son, but I'm damn sure you're not stuck here with me. As a matter of fact, you can jest turn your little gangster butt around and walk right back the way you came for all I care!"

"Sorry. I meant no disrespect, sir. Hey, Imma hella thirsty. You think you could hook a gangsta up with a drink a water? Or maybe one of dem beers?"

"Oh, I might be able to fix ya up with something cold to drink, alright. Might be able to mend that there wing of yers too. But only if ya start mindin' yer manners around here!"

"I'll mind 'em, sir."

The owl struggled to climb the three porch steps using its one good wing as the old man stood up from his rocker, opened the screen door, and disappeared into the dark of his house. He returned with a small plastic bowl, an unopened can of PBR, and a roll of veterinarian tape. He set the bowl on the porch, popped open the can, and poured some of the good stuff. Leaning over the edge of the bowl, the owl dipped its little beak into the white foam.

After the owl finished taking its drink, the old man gently picked the owl up and set it on the small table next to his rocker. He sat down to examine the bird's injured wing.

"Say, I thought ya said ya were shot. I don't see no bullet holes in this wing. Not even a cut. Looks like a normal break to me."

"I guess the gunshot wound musta healed up quick. I dunno. All I know is I was shot defendin' mah turf, yo."

"Hold still a second, little Owl Capone," the old man said as he ripped a 12-inch strip of tape off the roll. He carefully folded the owl's bad wing into the bird's side and wrapped the white tape around its body to hold the wing in place.

"Yer wing should mend alright as long as ya keep this bandage on for two weeks," the old man said. He grimaced, his jowly, wizened visage taking on an expression of suspicion. "Ya know what, Owl Capone? I bet yer from around these parts. Matter 'o fact, I bet you're prob'ly from those woods right there 'cross the road from me." He pointed across the street. "And I bet ya fell outta your mama's nest, broke yer wing, and that ya just watched too much TV in your nest before you fell out. Amiright?"

The owl hopped down off the table to get another draught of PBR. "You think what ya wanna think, old man." It dipped its beak into the beer again.

"Heh! I knew it! But you just go on right ahead and pretend whatever the hell you want to pretend, little fella. Heh. When I was yer age, we played games of pretend too, pretended we was soldiers and spies and pirates."

Along the road, a black Range Rover emerged from the woods that bordered the left side of the old man's hayfield, the gangsta rap bass booming from the luxury SUV's souped-up subwoofers, rattling the old man's dentures. Two riders hung partway out the front and back passenger-side windows while another rider popped up through the open sunroof. All three brandished assault rifles and wore bandanas that veiled their faces from just below the eyes down past their chins.

"There it is!" the gunman hanging out of sunroof shouted as the vehicle slowed down in front of the farmhouse. "Take its ass out for good this time!!"

"Get down, yo!" the owl cried. Both he and the old man dropped to the porch a split second before a hail of bullets pelted the house.

Curled up into fetal position, the old man wrapped his head in his arms as wood splintered and window panes shattered all around him. The fusillade lasted about thirty seconds before the Range Rover peeled out and way, careening around the bend in the road.

"Shit!" the old man blurted. Supine on the floorboards and spitting up blood, his frail body was perforated by several bullet holes. Groaning in pain, he rolled onto his belly and army-crawled over to where the owl lay motionless in its own pooling blood.

"I'm—I'm sorry, little Owl Capone," the old man said as he gently stroked the bloody feathers of the owl's head with his fingertips. "You're a for-real-ass, legit, THUG-4-LYFE gangster. I mean, gangSTA. I'm sorry. Sorry...I doubted you."

The partially shattered beak jutting out of the owl's face opened up. "Nah, old man. Don't you apologize for nothin'. I'm nothing but a pranksta. A perpetrata. A faka. A little, whack, punk-ass bitch. You were right before. Shit, I ain't never been to no Compton! I'm from across the road, just like you said. I'm just a regular country owl. The only thing I'm straight outta is the nest! Just like you said, I fell out and broke my wing. I ain't shit, yo."

"If...if that's true, then why did those gangsters just do a drive by on us? If they weren't after you, who were they after?"

"They were after me, pops," a voice said from nearby.

The old man rolled onto his back to see who had spoken. Someone—no, *something*—was standing—no *hovering*—near his front door. The old man squinted his eyes to see the thing better, to try to make out what it was.

"Are you...what I think you are?" the old man murmured.

"What do you think I am?" the voice said.

"I might be mistaken, but I think you might be that special pawn capture move in chess…shit, I can't seem to recall what it's called. You know, when a pawn moves forward two squares on its first move only to be captured by an opponent's pawn as if the first pawn had only moved forward one space."

"Holy shit!" the owl said. "Is that motherfuckin' en passant floating by your front door?"

"En passant!" the old man coughed. "That's what it's called! You're en passant, ain't ya!"

"In the flesh," en passant said. "Well, not in the flesh really, per se. But you are correct: I am the living, sentient embodiment of the chess move en passant."

"But why were those guys after you?" the old man asked.

"Because I killed a few of their boys," replied the special pawn move. "See, I recently grew tired of being a special pawn move in the game of chess. An en passant attack, like all other attacks in chess, is merely symbolic, symbolic in the sense that a player removes the attacked piece from the chessboard, sets it off to the side, and replaces it with the attacking piece. It's pure abstraction. An actual physical strike never takes place. Well, a few weeks ago, I decided to take a leave of absence from the game of chess and try my hand at some real violence, to see what it's like to rend real flesh and spill real blood."

"So do ya like real violence better than symbolic chess violence?" the old man asked.

"I have to say yes. I do indeed, old man."

"But I bet you only go after bad guys, right?" the owl asked.

"No, little owl," en passant said. "I'm afraid I'm not at all interested in making such morally relativistic distinctions. I'll fuck up an upstanding citizen just as soon as I'll fuck up a sociopathic criminal. I'll rip apart a newborn infant in front of its mother just as soon as I'll tear apart a serial killer."

"Dayum!" the owl said. "But you're not gonna hurt *us*, right? You're gonna call us an ambulance?"

"Sorry, little owl, but I'm afraid I'm not going to call you an ambulance. Yes, I *am* going to hurt both of you. To be perfectly candid with you, I'm about to tear this old man's wrinkled face off his skull like a cheap Halloween mask and then wrap you up in it like a baby in a blanket. Then, once you're all bundled up tight in his bloody face-flap, I'm gonna shove you straight up the old man's ass. But lucky for the both of you, you're all shot up and don't seem to be long for this world anyway. So I can't imagine either one of you is going to suffer too much longer regardless of what I do to you. I mean, imagine if I had gotten to you two when you weren't on the brink of death, when you were in relatively good health. Then you guys really would have been in trouble!"

"Yeah, I—I guess...we kinda lucked out in that respect," the old man said uncertainly.

"Yeah, yo," the owl agreed. "And at least we're going out like real gangstas."

"Well," en passant said, "if the drive by shooting had been the cause of your deaths, then yes, I suppose you could've boasted that you were going out like real gangstas. But now that I'm here to deliver the sadistic, horrific *coup de grâce* I've just described to you, you can't really say you're going out like gangstas anymore, can you? Now you're just going out like two very unlucky pieces of dried-out white dogshit."

"Hey, Imma just tryin' to keep things posi, yo," the owl said.

"I understand, little owl. I guess I'm just more about keepin' things real than keepin' things posi. Anyhow, I better get to work on peeling this old fella's face off before he dies on me and can't feel excruciating pain anymore."

Is Winona Ryder Still with the Dude from Soul Asylum?

"I'm tellin' you," en passant said as it examined its five-card poker hand, "Salieri was just as good as Mozart, if not better."

"Bullshit," I said as I slid a red poker chip to the middle of the upturned crate that served as a makeshift table in our bunker. "Then why is Mozart one of the most popular composers of all time, whereas Salieri is essentially a footnote in the history of classical music? Hell, if weren't for that lurid *Amadeus* movie, no one would even know Antonio Salieri ever existed."

"His operas from his middle and late Viennese periods are just as good as anything Mozart ever composed," en passant said as it flipped its ante into the betting pile. "I actually attended many of Salieri's premieres, ya know."

This claim was probably true. En passant had been around for a long time. En passant had been all over the world. In fact, en passant had been everywhere in the world where chessboards and chess players had ever existed. As a special pawn move in the game of chess, en passant was as old as the game itself—about fifteen-hundred years by most scholars' reckoning. And from the stories it told me, en passant had seen some serious shit in its day—the rise and fall of empires, the exploration of the globe, all the great wars and paradigm shifts of the Common Era. Still, just because the thing had seen a lot of shit didn't mean it also had good taste in opera.

"C'mon," I said. "*The Magic Flute*. *Don Giovanni*. *The Marriage of Figaro*. That stuff is timeless. Sublime. Name one Salieri opera that's better than any one of those?"

"*La Fiera di Venezia*."

"*La Fiera di Venezia*! You kiddin' me? Yeah, so *La Fiera* was the first opera to ever feature vocal dances for both the actors *and* the chorus. But at what cost? *La Fiera* was clearly a case of compromising compositional integrity for the sake of spectacle. Does that clusterfuck of an opera even have one memorable melody buried deep within it somewhere? Not one I can remember."

"We can agree to disagree then," en passant said politely as it laid two of its cards facedown and pushed them next to the deck.

Since it was my turn to deal, I pinched the top two cards off the deck and set them facedown near en passant's chip stack.

The special pawn move picked up the two new cards and merged them with the rest of its hand. Being the material manifestation of an abstract concept, en passant had no face of which to speak. And what poker face was better than no face at all? In fact, the only visual evidence that this pawn move incarnate did indeed sit across from me was a disturbance in the air on the opposite side of the crate, like a heat haze radiating off a stretch of sunbaked blacktop. Well, that and the big-ass sombrero en passant wore, which appeared to float in the air above said hazy disturbance. Nevertheless, I could hold my own against en passant in most card games. In fact, I was up two hundred smackeroonies in our present contest.

"So Salieri's operas don't do much for ya," en passant said, "but what about his other stuff?"

"What other stuff? Do you mean his pitifully short and forgettable catalog of mediocre chamber music and sacred music?"

"No, I mean his song 'Is Winona Ryder Still with the Dude from Soul Asylum?'"

Slack-jawed, I closed my eyes and let my head drop while shaking it. "Ohhh, shit! I forgot he even wrote that!"

In case you're not in the know, the song "Is Winona Ryder Still with the Dude from Soul Asylum?" was the first gangsta rap song ever written and recorded.

Ever.

And not only did Salieri write the lyrics to the song, he also rapped them himself during the song's original recording way back in 1773. The lyrics of "Is Winona Ryder Still with the Dude from Soul Asylum?" touched on such themes as pimping hos, protecting your turf in Compton, California from rival gangstas, hustling dope, slappin' hos to keep them in line, unchecked and unapologetic materialism and hedonism, killing cops, killing and cannibalizing the wives and children of the cops you killed, having sex with corpses to show how gangsta you were, eating SpaghettiOs sandwiches made with Wonder Bread, burying Chicken McNuggets in tiny Chicken McNugget-shaped coffins in your front yard and having funerals for them, devouring handfuls of squirming worms and maggots just for fun, reading Kierkegaard translated from the original

Danish to ancient Greek cuz you just don't give a heck, and all kinds of other gangsta shit.

Point being, dude was waaaaaay ahead of his time. Shit, Salieri was rapping about being a gangsta in Compton before Compton was even on the map! The United States wasn't even around when he composed that song! Salieri played the synth tracks and programmed the fresh drum beat featured in the tune, all done before synthesizers and drum machines even existed! How is that even fucking possible? Equally astounding, Salieri wrote and recorded the song before the ability to record music even existed!

Yup, I'd totally forgotten that Salieri was actually pretty hardcore. I now I found myself feeling not a small amount embarrassment about this lapse in my memory—I, who took so much pride in my self-proclaimed encyclopedic knowledge of all things music.

"Man, I can't believe I forgot Salieri wrote and recorded 'Is Winona Ryder Still with the Dude from Soul Asylum?' Alright, so maybe Salieri was better than Mozart."

"Now you're talkin' sense," en passant said. "And I'll bet ya twenty, friend." The special pawn move pushed two ten-dollar chips to the middle of the crate. As it did so, the ground above us began to tremble. The solitary light bulb dangling from the ceiling shook. Our stacks of poker chips toppled over, and the fallen chips rattled atop the quavering crate. It was as if we were in the midst of an earthquake. But it wasn't an earthquake.

It was the annual Stampede of the Loop-Puppets.

The Stampede of the Loop-Puppets happened every year on July 42th, usually occurring around fuck o'clock and lasting for about fifteen to twenty minutes. The Stampede was the reason en passant and I had holed ourselves down in this bunker several hours ago, because the only way to survive it was to get underground. But a basement, even a securely locked one, wouldn't do the trick. The Loop-Puppets would get you if you tried to hide in a basement. Your only hope was to get yourself into a steel-reinforced concrete bunker with a military-grade blast hatch that had a pressure rating of at least 92.58 PSI. Anything less than 92.58 PSI and you were pretty much fucked—those ravenous fiends would pry the hatch off, pour in like starving rats, and reduce you and your family to screaming, bloody skeletons within seconds.

No one knew what Loop-Puppets looked like because no one had ever seen them and lived to tell about it. All attempts at capturing the Loop-Puppets on film had only ever yielded unidentifiable, featureless streaks of motion streaming across the ground.

I glanced down at my watch. "It's happening a little early this year."

"Oh, yeah? What time is it?"

"Still only few minutes until shit o'clock."

"It's not even shit o'clock yet? Wow. Are you sure? Seems like just a minute it ago it was cunt hat o'clock already."

"Yeah, I'm sure. Time always drags when you're holed up in one of these bunkers. At any rate, earlier is better than later, right? That's less time we have to wait."

Though I knew we were perfectly safe, that didn't make the Stampede any less nerve wracking, especially when, over the constant rumble above us, I distinctly heard those bloodthirsty imps pausing above our bunker from time to time to test the integrity of our hatch, pounding and scratching, prying their fingers along its edges.

"I fold," I said, laying my cards down on the crate. I didn't have a good high card, and I wasn't in the mood to bluff.

En passant invisibly grabbed its meager winnings, pulled them back to its rattling pool of chips.

"Hey," en passant said, "speaking of 'Is Winona Ryder Still with the Dude from Soul Asylum?', do you know if Winona Ryder is still with the dude from Soul Asylum?"

"I don't think so. I think they broke up back in the 90s, but I'm not sure."

"You should ask Siri."

I picked up my iPhone, pressed the on button. "Siri, is Winona Ryder still with the dude from Soul Asylum?"

"Yes," Siri said in her choppy robot voice. "On July 42th 1996, both Winona Ryder and the dude from Soul Asylum inexplicably turned into one-foot tall wooden puppet versions of themselves. Then, via binary fission, they rapidly reproduced until there were trillions and trillions of evil Winona Ryder puppets and evil the-dude-from-Soul-Asylum puppets. Winona Ryder and the dude from Soul Asylum *ARE THE LOOP-PUPPETS!*"

En passant and I both laughed.

"Siri must be broken or something," en passant said.

"Haha, yeah. Or maybe the newest version of Siri is programmed to tell jokes."

En passant and I sat around without speaking for a while, listening to the steady rumble above, to the scratching, the pounding, and the prying of little fingers at the hatch. We were waiting out the Stampede like we'd done every July 42th since we could remember. It would be over in a few minutes. Nevertheless, the lull in our conversation made this loud "silence" more tense.

"So where did you get that sombrero from?" I asked en passant just to get the conversation going again.

"Felipe."

Felipe was a merciless drug cartel boss who had illegally immigrated to the U.S. from Mexico and moved into the house next door to us about two months ago.

"Oh, cool. Did he give it to you as gift?"

"No, I made a trade with him a few days ago."

"What did you trade him?"

"Well, he offered me his sombrero if I gave him our 92.58-PSI blast hatch for his 92.57-PSI blast hatch. Seemed like a pretty sweet deal. It's a real Mexican sombrero handmade made by old Mexican ladies. Pretty slick, huh?"

"Did you just say you traded our 92.58-PSI bunker hatch for a 92.57-PSI bunker hatch?" I uttered in disbelief.

"Yup."

"Oh, shit."

"What?"

"Ya fucked up, en passant. Big time."

"Whaddaya mean?"

That's when the deadbolt assembly that held our hatch shut snapped under the tremendous forces pulling at it. The hatch flipped up and away, ripped from its hinges.

I clamped my eyes shut and braced myself, expecting the Loop-Puppets to pour in and shred us to bits. But that's not what happened. At least not yet.

"Are there any negroes, Chinamen, Latinos, or Jews hiding down there?" a male voice with a stuffy, old-fashioned-sounding New England accent asked loudly over the continuing rumble of the Stampede.

I opened my eyes and glanced up at the hatch. Fuckin' H.P. Lovecraft and Martin "Pharma Bro" Shkreli were looking down at us through the square hole in our ceiling. Shouldering an assault rifle, Lovecraft clenched one eye shut as he drew a bead on my fat face.

"Um, no, Mr. Lovecraft," I said, putting my hands up in the air. "It's just me and en passant. There's no one else down here."

"You sure?" Lovecraft asked, not taking his aim off me.

"Yeah, yeah, I'm sure. You can come down and check for yourself if you want."

A moment passed before the racist Father of Cosmic Horror said, "Okay." Satisfied, he lowered the barrel of the rifle and slung the firearm over his shoulder.

"Hey, do either of you have AIDS?" Pharma Bro asked.

"No," we both said.

"No?" Pharma Bro said. "Well, do you wanna buy some of the most effective AIDS medicine available on the market anyway? Just in case you get AIDS in the future? I can sell you both a bottle." The universally hated man held up two amber pill vials and shook them like maracas.

"How much?" I asked.

"Nine hundred thousand dollars and three cents per bottle."

"Sorry," I said. "We only have about a couple hundred bucks between the two of us."

"Then I guess you lose, fag. Hey, H.P., let's keep moving, brah."

Pharma Bro and H.P. Lovecraft then withdrew from the square hole in the ceiling. In their stead, the Loop-Puppets began to pour in.

Siri was right: The Loop-Puppets were one-foot tall wooden puppet versions of Winona Ryder and the dude from Soul Asylum. I clenched my eyes shut again, steeling myself for a painful but hopefully quick death.

One of the Loop-Puppets hopped on my chest, grabbed me by the collar, and shook my head all around like it was nothing. I opened my eyes to find myself staring into the face of one of the dude-from-Soul-Asylum puppets.

"Say my name, fuckhead!" it cried. "Say my name and maybe we'll let you two live!"

"Uh…um...your name is…it's…your name is…the dude from Soul Asylum?"

"That's not my name, dick! Prepare to die!"

"No, please, wait!" I begged. "En passant, do you know what his name is?"

"All I know is he's the dude from Soul Asylum," the special chess move said. "Shit, I don't think I ever heard his name before."

"Wait, wait, wait!" I said. "Let me ask Siri. Siri, what is the name of the lead singer of—"

One of the countless Winona Ryder puppets that now occupied the bunker smashed my cell phone onto the floor.

"No cheating," the thing hissed at me.

"Okay, okay, I remember your name!" I lied. I had to at least take a guess, right? It was our last hope. "Your name is…"

"Well, what is it?" scores of Winona Ryder puppets and the-dude-from-Soul-Asylum puppets said in chorus.

"Your name is…aw, fuck. I don't know what your goddamn name is. I bet your own mother doesn't what your name is, you burned-out, has-been, C-list, all-but-forgotten, quasi-celebrity! I bet you work at fucking Taco Bell nowadays. FUCK YOU, THE DUDE FROM SOUL ASYLUM!!!"

That, of course, wasn't what the Loop-Puppets wanted to hear.

But hey, at least we went out like motherfuckin' gangstas.

Betta ask somebody.

THE END

P.S. Not many people know this, but prior to the Loop-Puppets skeletonizing us, en passant got mad ass.

Which, of course, wasn't fair at all. En passant wasn't even human, yet the pawn move still managed to score more cream of the crop, supermodel-grade, Victoria's Secret model-like, NFL cheerleader-caliber ass than a boyband. Me, I got laid like maybe three or four times in my thirty-five years on this planet. What a waste of eight inches of limp whitesnake.

I have no idea why I am complaining about this now considering I'm deader than a piece of dried-out white dogshit vaporized by a 500-kiloton nuclear bomb. Perhaps I only mention it as warning to *you*, dear reader.

Yes: Seize the day, people! To hell with your shyness, your insecurities, and, if applicable, your unrealistic standards (no, we can't all be an ass-tappin' special pawn moves like en passant.) Once you're dead, you'll have all eternity to be shy and insecure while holding all the unrealistic standards you want. So get out there and nab as much ass and/or cock as you can before you're deader than piece of dried-out white dogshit vaporized by a 500-kiloton nuclear bomb.

Carpe diem, yo!

P.P.S. Okay, so maybe you already get mad ass, and the above advice doesn't apply to you. Well, then all I have to say is don't let all that ass get to your head and make ya stupid, son! Because that's what happened to en passant. That's why en passant forgot that the pressure rating of a blast hatch on a Stampede of the Loop-Puppets bunker has to be at least 92.58 PSI.

Dumbass!

Well, at any rate, so long. It's back to The Void for me!

The Many Bad Habits of My Main Man, Klin-Klat, A.K.A. the Tap Dance Kid

Klin-Klat had many bad habits, one of which was crashing closed casket funerals in order to hop up onto strangers' coffins and announce, "Back in the day, they used to call me the motherfuckin' Tap Dance Kid!" just before he'd tap dance on the lid.

However, my main man never got very far into his coffin-top dance routines, his pointy tap dancing shoes usually only executing a few *tippety-taps* before the angry mourners and funeral parlor staff came charging after him, forcing him to climb down and make his escape while gleefully repeating his own name in his signature babyish, singsong voice.

"Klin-Klat! Klin-Klat! Klin-Klat! Klin-Klat..."

Dude also smoked three packs of cigarettes a day.

Another one of Klin-Klat's bad habits was crashing *open* casket funerals for the purpose of climbing inside people's coffins to say, "Back in the day, they used to call me the motherfuckin' Tap Dance Kid!" before tap dancing on the faces of the deceased. Like the closed casket incidents, such intrusions invariably ended in chase, my main man always chanting, "Klin-Klat! Klin-Klat! Klin-Klat..." as he booked for the exit.

Klin-Klat also picked his nose a lot in public.

Dude ate his boogers too. And he didn't care if people saw him do it.

Yet another one of Klin-Klat's bad habits was breaking into hospices in order to climb onto the heads of dying people while shouting, "Back in the day, they used to call me the motherfuckin' Tap Dance Kid!" After delivering his catch-phrase, Klin-Klat would tap dance on the moribund person's face, usually hastening the patient's already imminent demise. Just like the funeral crashes, such trespasses always ended with my main man getting chased off the premises.

He also chewed his fingernails down to the quick whenever he was nervous.

Still another one of Klin-Klat's bad habits was breaking into maternity wards to tap dance on infants, typically just after they were pulled from their mothers' birth canals. My main man would shout, "Back in the day, they used to call me the motherfuckin' Tap Dance Kid!" as he did so, of course. Just three or four smart taps with those spiffy shoes of his was all it took to effectively churn such ill-starred newborns into baby-jam, those startled doctors and nurses never getting much of a chance to react to my main man's unexpected intrusion.

"Klin-Klat! Klin-Klat! Klin-Klat..." he'd sing as he was chased out of the hospital.

Whenever my main man conversed with anyone, he continually interrupted them. Dude cussed like a sailor. Drank way too much. Spent too much time watching TV and playing video games (and he sat like two inches away from the TV screen when he did so). Skipped breakfast every morning. Ate greasy fast food for lunch and dinner every day. Chewed with his mouth open. Gambled his paychecks away. Abused sundry street drugs and any prescription meds he could get his mitts on. Went to bed late every night. Said "um" and "like" too much. Didn't bathe, comb his hair, brush his teeth, or floss. Liked to pick at his scabs too.

    Okay, so my main man was not without his flaws. But who isn't? Are you without flaws, bruh? And what about you, sis? Are you a perfect person? No, I didn't think so.

    Yes, Klin-Klat was far from perfect. But I'll tell ya what: While my main man certainly was not the most admirable person in the world, dude could tap dance like it was nobody's motherfuckin' business!

    In fact, back in the day, they used to call my man the motherfuckin' Tap Dance Kid!!!!!!!!!!!

This Puppet Puts the "P" in "Puppet"

I had just sat down at my kitchen table to enjoy a lunch of boiled tip-taps, poached foo-faps, and fried pop-dots when a bright knock sounded at my front door.

Must be Crub, I thought as I dabbed my lips with a napkin, set the napkin on the table, and stood up from my chair.

The nameless country road on which I lived was quite remote and only had four houses on it. There was my old but well-kept farmhouse, Crub's double-wide prefab across the street from me and, just a short stroll down the road from our houses, two dilapidated structures that sat across from one another on either side of a dead end. Of the latter two dwellings, the one on Crub's side was inhabited by the Gray Puppet. The decrepit villa directly across from the Gray Puppet's house was vacant, the residence's last occupant—a puppet named Belloh-Bellah the Funtime-TERROR-Effigy—having abandoned the place many years ago to go travel the world.

To our knowledge, the Gray Puppet had not stepped out of its house in seven years, so a knock on my front door, irrespective of time of day or night, left little doubt in my mind that I'd find old Crub standing out on my front porch. I, of course, counted this among the chief benefits of living in such a secluded place (i.e., the almost complete lack of visitors and solicitors). The only thing I liked more about living there was perhaps the absence of any and all mail.

Still, one could never be too careful. So when I reached my front door that day, I put an eye to the peephole to confirm it was him.

Indeed, it was. The eighty-year-old man's grizzled, foot-long white beard was fluttering in the wind, his grubby t-shirt as grubby as ever (the fading block letters on the shirt read, WHILE I'M STILL ALIVE, PLEASE DON'T BURN MY SKIN WITH MATCHES. AND AFTER I'M DEAD AND BURIED, PLEASE DON'T DIG UP MY BODY A YEAR LATER, MAKE FUN OF IT, AND POKE IT WITH A STICK!), and his thick, cracked, eye-magnifying bifocals were as thick, cracked, and eye-magnifying as ever.

"Hi, Crub," I said after I unlocked and opened the door, the savory aroma of Chicken McNuggets instantly filling my nostrils.

"We have a new neighbor," the old man said, his gnarled facial expression a mixture of seriousness and bottled excitement. In one tremulous, arthritic hand, he grasped a 20-piece box of Chicken McNuggets. With his other hand, he pointed toward the end of our street.

I leaned out the doorway, turned my head to look in that direction.

Sure enough, a moving truck was backing out of the driveway of the old house where Belloh-Bellah the Funtime-TERROR-Effigy used to live. The words "Two Mannequins and a Truck" were emblazoned across its side.

Crub and I watched the truck as it rolled slowly down the street toward us. One mannequin drove the vehicle while another sat in the passenger seat. They both waved at us with stiff alabaster arms as the truck passed by.

We waved back.

"Did you see who moved in?" I asked as we watched the truck turn off our byway onto a road that, but for the fact that it eventually wound its way back to a state route and had somesuch name or other, was as far removed from the rest of the world as our own.

"Not *who* moved in, but *what*," Crub said. "I saw it this morning. It was out on the porch when the movers were moving its stuff in. I went over to say hey."

If our new neighbor was a "what" and not a "who," that meant the neighbor was either a mannequin or a puppet.

"Well, what is it?" I asked.

"It's a puppet."

"What's this puppet's name?"

"It doesn't have a name."

I raised an incredulous eyebrow.

"I asked it what its name is," Crub said. "It said it doesn't have one."

"What kind of puppet doesn't have a name?"

"The great kind."

"Great? What do you mean? How great?"

"Greater than any puppet you've ever encountered before."

"Greater than Belloh-Bellah the Funtime-TERROR-Effigy?"

"Way greater than Belloh-Bellah. In fact, I'd go as far to say that this puppet puts the 'p' in 'puppet.'"

That was saying a lot, as Belloh-Bellah the Funtime-TERROR-Effigy was just about as great as a puppet—or a person or a mannequin for that matter—could be. Not only could

Belloh-Bellah play the violin like Paganini, sing opera like Pavarotti, paint like Rembrandt, and tap dance like Fred Astaire, it cooked like Emeril and was a generous host to boot. Thus, I was understandably skeptical to hear tell of a puppet greater than the great Belloh-Bellah.

"Bullshit," I said. "No puppet is better than Belloh-Bellah. What makes this new puppet so special?"

"It's hard to explain, but I guarantee you'll agree." Crub held up the box of Chicken McNuggets. "I'm going to bring it this welcome gift. Come with me, and I'll introduce you."

Just about any prepared food—casseroles, pastas, pies, cookies, et al—were suitable welcome gifts when humans moved onto one's street. But when a puppet moved in, one would be remiss if within three or four days one did not show up at the puppet's doorstep with a 20-piece order of Chicken McNuggets. That's all puppets ever ate, notwithstanding the advanced culinary skills some of them possessed and showed off just for the benefit of their human friends.

"Very well," I said. "I shall go with you. And I shall judge for myself if this puppet does indeed put the 'p' in 'puppet'!"

***

The stroll from my house to the dead end of our road took only about half a minute. We had to walk in the road itself to avoid the dense stretch of brambles and sumac that separated my well-manicured lawn from the high, weedy grass of our new neighbor's property. Just before we turned up its driveway, I paused and glanced across the street toward the Gray Puppet's house, raising my gaze to the attic dormer window. As I expected, the Gray Puppet's glowing eyes—two little pinpoints of red hellfire—stared down at us from the black gloom of that high rectangle.

As far as we knew, the Gray Puppet had not moved from its perch in that window since we ostracized it from our company seven years ago. Crub and I had once been good friends with it. But one afternoon, the three of us met for a picnic lunch (of Chicken McNuggets) on the Gray Puppet's front lawn as we were wont to do back in those days, when, completely unprovoked, the Gray Puppet stood up and scratched Crub's arm with his little plastic hand, drawing blood. Shocked, we scolded it for this uncharacteristic act of aggression and unkindness. The thing responded by lurching after me in an attempt to scratch *my* arm as well! Luckily, I rolled out of harm's way. Crub and I then grabbed the blanket and what remained of our Chicken McNugget lunch and ran back to my house.

"Fuck you, the Gray Puppet!" Crub yelled over his shoulder as we escaped, leaving the thing standing in its front yard like some sort of grotesque gray lawn ornament. Soon after, this bad puppet retreated into the darkness of its house, where it took up a lookout post in its attic window. To our knowledge, the Gray Puppet had neither left its house nor pulled itself away from that attic window since that time.

Now, as I stared up at those two demonic dots in the window, I couldn't help but recall when we brought a welcome gift of Chicken McNuggets to the Gray Puppet just after it moved onto our street some fifteen years ago, long before the puppet ever became an arm-scratching asshole.

Crub glanced up at the window too. "What are you looking at, fucker?" he called to the Gray Puppet as he flipped it the bird before turning away and continuing up our new neighbor's drive. I turned to follow him. As we neared the house, I still felt the Gray Puppet's shuddersome gaze on my back.

After we climbed the steps to the front porch, Crub knocked thrice on the door.

A moment later, the door swung inward to reveal a forlorn darkness comparable to that of the Gray Puppet's attic window. The Nameless Puppet, which is what we later came to call our new neighbor, appeared a beat later.

Standing about two feet tall, it was dressed in an antique Little Lord Fauntleroy suit complete with a filigree laced collar, a puffy blouse, knee-length pants trimmed with lace, fancy white stockings, and black patent strap shoes. Though fire had at some point in the past destroyed most of the puppet's plastic head and face, one could imagine the cherubic contours, dimpled cheeks, and rosebud lips its little visage must have once boasted. Now charred blackness replaced most of the pink flesh tone of the head. The only surviving feature of the face's former beauty was a single long-lashed glass eye of brilliant cornflower blue.

The Nameless Puppet stepped over the threshold and stopped mere inches from my feet. It leaned back to look up at me with its single eye. "Hello," it said in a high-pitched, childlike timbre. Like other puppets and mannequins, it communicated telepathically.

"Hello," I said.

"This is Lancelot-Ahncelot Jenkins," Crub said to the puppet. "He lives in the house across from mine. We brought you these Chicken McNuggets."

The Nameless Puppet continued to stare up at me. "Please don't be an unkind man to me," it said. "And please don't be cross with me."

I leaned down, grasped the Nameless Puppet under its arms, and lifted it into the air as if the thing were my own child. "I would never think of being unkind to you, precious poppet," I said. "And you've certainly given me no reason to be cross." I embraced it and kissed each of its cheeks before gently setting it back down onto its feet.

Satisfied that I was friend and not foe, it turned to Crub and held out its little arms to receive its gift.

"Follow me, my new friends," it said as it took the box of Chicken McNuggets from Crub and waddled down the porch steps.

We followed it through the tall grass to the center of the front yard, where a wide, round clearing had been recently mowed, calling to mind a crop circle. Near the center of the circle was a cluster of rectangular holes, each about the size of a playing card. Small mounds of displaced earth were scattered between the holes. Beside each hole was an even smaller, wooden container. Due to the tapered hexagonal shape of these little vessels, I had to assume they were miniature coffins. I then noticed a loose stack of tiny crosses on the other side of these diminutive...*graves*? The crosses had been fashioned from twigs tied together with string.

What purpose could such tiny coffins and graves serve? I wondered. *To bury baby birds? Mice? Toads?*

As if to answer my unspoken question, the Nameless Puppet removed the lid from one of the coffins, revealing its empty interior. It then reached into the box of Chicken McNuggets, grabbed a McNugget, and placed it inside the open coffin before fitting the lid back on. It then set the coffin carefully into its grave.

We watched in stunned silence as the Nameless Puppet repeated this process nineteen times.

Twenty graves for twenty Chicken McNuggets.

As this was happening, Crub nudged my arm.

I turned to look at the old man. He grinned and nodded as if to say *I told you this puppet puts the "p" in "puppet"!*

"My friends," the Nameless Puppet said when it was finished, "would you assist me in filling in these graves?"

"Of course we will, delightful poppet," I said.

The Nameless Puppet took a small shovel and began to fill in a grave. For our part, Crub and I dropped to our hands and knees and used our hands to do the same. After filling in all the little graves, we helped the puppet place the twig crosses at the heads of each.

This mass burial of Chicken McNuggets was probably the greatest thing to ever happen to me. I certainly could not think of another puppet who had ever done anything so singularly wonderful. Unfortunately, my enjoyment of the occasion was tainted somewhat by the creepy, gooseflesh-inducing sensation of the Gray Puppet's eyes shamelessly staring down at us from its accursed attic window the entire time, as if we had gathered below it for the banished puppet's own voyeuristic entertainment. I refused to look up at the window until after we finished. When I did look, I shook my fist in the air.

"You're not even half the puppet this puppet is!" I shouted at those terrible red eyes. "Fuck you, the Gray Puppet! Fuck you!"

"Yeah, fuck you, the Gray Puppet!" Crub echoed. "This puppet puts the 'p' in 'puppet'! You, you put the 'a' in 'asshole'!" He gave the Gray Puppet the finger again before hoisting the Nameless Puppet up onto his shoulders like Tiny Tim. We then walked back to the Nameless Puppet's house.

***

I really cannot sing the praises of the Nameless Puppet enough.

Now granted, the tea it brewed for us when we visited its house was often lukewarm and insipid, and the little cakes it baked for us were always dry and crumbly. Sure, when it played the violin to entertain us, its wild sawings sounded like a cat being flayed alive, while its shrill, off-key singing voice was no less torturous to endure. Whenever it sat at the easel with its paints and brushes, the Nameless Puppet produced only the most unappealing, simplistic, childlike abstractions. With the exception of the occasional crudely rendered smiley face, all such canvases consisted of nothing more than random swirls, smudges, and smears of arbitrarily selected colors, even when the puppet attempted to realistically depict, say, a bowl of fruit, a landscape, or our portraits. The thing's attempts at tap dancing were pathetic, at best unintentionally humorous, and I wouldn't have wished its mealtime cooking on the Gray Puppet itself.

Yet we never complained, ridiculed, or tried to correct the Nameless Puppet's shortcomings or deficiencies in any way. On the contrary, we complimented everything it did for us, tolerated its performances with patience, and consumed its gag-inducing culinary creations without ever once pulling a sour face.

The reason our patience with the Nameless Puppet knew no bounds was that every time we brought Chicken McNuggets to its house, instead of a picnic, we had a mass burial, so that within a just a few months, the Nameless Puppet's entire front lawn was transformed into a Chicken McNuggets graveyard! But our fun did not end there. When we ran out of space in the front yard, we began burying the things on either side of the puppet's house and then in the five-acre field that was its backyard.

And what the Nameless Puppet lacked in artistic, musical, and culinary talent, it more than made up for with its carpentry and blacksmithing skills, as the puppet fashioned every one of those tiny coffins itself using wood hewn on its very own carpentry bench and nails cast and hammered at its very own forge, both of which were kept in its basement.

I mean, what other puppet ever built tiny coffins and dug little graves for Chicken McNuggets? What's more, the puppet engaged in this ritual not as some type of protest against killing animals for food, but rather just for the sake of doing it.

Truly, the Nameless Puppet had to be the greatest puppet in the world!!!

***

My thirtieth birthday fell on a day almost exactly nine months after the Nameless Puppet moved onto our equally nameless road. I had never been fond of birthdays, particularly my own. As such, in the days prior to my thirtieth, I did not even bother telling Crub or the Nameless Puppet it was coming up. However, Crub and I did make plans that day to visit the Nameless Puppet in our usual fashion. And if truth be told, I could not ask for a better birthday present than to spend the afternoon burying Chicken McNuggets with the two of them, followed by an evening of the many flawed though no less charming entertainments provided by our diminutive host.

I was sitting in my drawing room listening to Debussy on the gramophone, waiting for Crub to show up with the Chicken McNuggets when, just as the record ended, I barely discerned a knock coming from my front door. This muted sound—really more of a tapping—surely did not belong to Crub, whose bony knuckles always rapped on the oak of my front door with an impressive force. When I looked through the peephole a moment later, it appeared no one was out there, yet still I heard that faint tapping.

Perhaps it is the Nameless Puppet, I wondered.

But when I opened the door, I was shocked to discover a Chicken McNugget standing at my feet. The thing had sprouted little stick figure arms and legs, googly eyes, and a small o-shaped mouth so that it resembled some manner of stop-animation figure. I could only assume this Chicken

McNugget had somehow managed to escape its grave next door.

"Little McNugget," I said as I bent down and rested my palms on my thighs, "what hath disturbed thy eternal sleep?"

"The Gray Puppet!" the thing squeaked. "It killed the Nameless Puppet! And it killed Crub! And it dug up all the McNuggets and ate them! I was the only one to escape!"

Without hesitation, I grabbed the loaded shotgun I kept in the foyer closet, flew out of my front door and down the porch steps, and made for the street. As I sprinted down the middle of the road and drew nearer to the dead end, I spotted the Gray Puppet dragging itself across its porch to its open door, its Chicken McNugget-stuffed belly swollen to ten times its normal size, its eyes burning with extra ferocity, its elvish, hook-nosed face and hands scarlet with fresh, slick blood. When I came to a breathless stop between the two houses, the Gray Puppet slammed the door shut behind it before I could draw a bead on the accursed thing's head.

In shock and horror, I approached the Nameless Puppet's yard with slow, shaky footsteps. Those thousands of Chicken McNugget graves had indeed been unearthed, every last one of them. With nary a Chicken McNugget in sight, the yard was now dotted with holes and littered with empty tiny coffins, tiny coffin lids, and trampled twig crosses.

"Cr-r-Crub," I stammered.

What remained of the old man lay scattered before me near the curb. The Gray Puppet had literally torn him to shreds. The only reason I knew this steaming pile of blood, guts, flesh, bone, skin, shit, piss, semen, bile, chyme, chyle, and tears in front of me was my former neighbor was the foot-long white beard that stuck out of it, fluttering like a fallen flag of surrender, along with a bloody shred of t-shirt that read, PLEASE DON'T BURN MY SKIN WITH MATCHES.

My gaze moved past Crub's remains to the center of the yard, where something black and charred lay, something still smoking from the fire that had just consumed it, something shaped like a two-foot-tall person.

"The Nameless Puppet..." I whispered as I fell to my knees, not caring that I was now kneeling in the pulpy gore that had once been old Crub, the only other human being on Earth I had ever been able to endure sitting in the same room with.

"No, God, why!" I cried and shook my fists at the sky, my face awash with tears. "Alack and cursed be the day that some puppet maker saw it fit to make the Gray Puppet!"

As hot tears rained down my face, I let my gaze drop from the steel-colored sky to the steel in my hands.

I stared at the shotgun for a good long minute.

"Good-bye, cruel world," I said before inserting the end of its barrel into my mouth. My finger on the trigger, I clenched my eyes shut and...squeezed.

CLICK.

But no *BOOM!*

"HAPPY BIRTHDAY!" a chorus of voices then shouted behind me, erupting into a joyful burst of cheers, hoots, hollers, and laughter.

I opened my eyes, yanked the shotgun barrel from my lips, and turned to look over my shoulder.

Standing on the Gray Puppet's lawn was basically everyone in the world I knew. Crub and the Nameless Puppet were there, both very much alive and unharmed. Crub's grubby t-shirt and even grubbier beard were still intact. The Gray Puppet, who was now removing the fake distended stomach it had worn to play its part in the elaborate prank, was there too. Surrounding them were thousands of disinterred Chicken McNuggets, all with arms, legs, twinkling eyes, and little o-shaped mouths, all of them holding "Happy Birthday!" balloons in all the colors of the rainbow. Even the two mannequins from Two Mannequins and a Truck were there. And standing between them...*could it really be?*

Grinning wide, I dropped the gun, pushed myself to my feet. "Belloh-Bellah?" I uttered in disbelief.

Belloh-Bellah the Funtime-TERROR-Effigy stepped forward from between the two mannequins. In its upturned hands, the clown-like puppet held a birthday cake topped with thirty burning candles. "Yes, it's me, old friend!" it said, the prodigal puppet returned. "Happy Birthday, Lancelot-Ahncelot!"

"We tricked you, Lancelot-Ahncelot!" the Nameless Puppet said, its voice rife with wicked glee and mischief.

"We even replaced the shells in your shotgun with empties!" Crub said.

"Yeah, I noticed. But...but what about the Gray Puppet?" I asked, confused.

"The Gray Puppet and I have been in on this for seven years now," Crub said. "We started planning your thirtieth birthday when you were twenty-three."

"You mean when the Gray Puppet attacked us seven years ago and then locked itself up in its attic for the better part of a decade...that was all part of the plan?"

"Yes," Crub said. "We wanted you to think the Gray Puppet was a fucking asshole, the sort of puppet that would kill people and puppets and violate the graves of Chicken McNuggets."

My head still reeling, I was having a hard time accepting it all. "You mean the Gray Puppet is *not* a complete fucking asshole?" I blurted.

"I'm not," the Gray Puppet said. "I'm actually a very kind puppet. I'm chill as hell. In fact, I'm so chill, I'm like the chillmaster of Chillville."

"But what about all this blood and guts?" I asked, gesturing at the ground. "I was sure this was you, Crub."

"Well," Crub said, pointing at the long beard sticking out of the red mess, "the fake *Duck Dynasty* beard you see there, we picked that up at Walmart, and the t-shirt I found on eBay. The rest is just SpaghettiOs with Meatballs." That last remark prompted everyone present—puppet, man, mannequin, and Chicken McNugget alike—to burst into a chorus of laughter. "Yep, about fifty family-size cans worth!"

"Holy shit!" I cried, half-insane. "This has to be the best surprise birthday party ever!"

***

It is not my intention to bore you with the details of the massive cleanup that followed my thirtieth birthday party, but I suppose I must at least make mention of it. For one, we had to return thousands of exhumed Chicken McNuggets to their little graves. But while some of the McNuggets were content to be buried alive a second time, others asked to be killed prior to reburial. Of course, we didn't have the heart to kill them ourselves, so we purchased thousands of miniature shotguns so that any McNugget wishing to blow its own fucking brains out could do so.

But that wasn't even the half of it.

We also had to dig *hundreds of thousands* of even tinier graves for each and every one of the SpaghettiOs and meatballs that had been spilled onto the Nameless Puppet's front lawn. During my birthday party, each circular noodle and gray meatball had sprouted limbs, eyes, and mouths of its own, all demanding the same treatment as the McNuggets. And like the McNuggets, not every noodle and meatball was keen on the idea of being buried alive. Unfortunately, however, the shotguns used by the McNuggets were too large for the SpaghettiOs and meatballs to handle, so we were obligated to purchase hundreds of thousands of *even smaller* shotguns—shotguns the meatballs could handle, and even smaller ones for the SpaghettiOs—thereby allowing those who wished to do so to blow their fucking brains out prior to being buried. Of course, this mass burial of SpaghettiOs and meatballs required the Nameless Puppet to fashion hundreds of thousands of additional miniature coffins. The rest of us helped by making as many twig crosses and digging as many teeny tiny graves.

These labors might have been manageable if it had not been for the many McNuggets, SpaghettiOs, and meatballs who demanded *their own individual funerals*, funerals complete with catering, expensive flower arrangements, mourners, and a priest to say funeral rites over their graves. Luckily, we knew a reclusive half-mannequin, half-marionette ordained priest who lived out in the woods beyond our road's dead end who agreed to officiate over the funeral services. Indeed, we were also lucky in that I was the beneficiary of a nearly inexhaustible trust fund, so money was not an object. At first, the Nameless Puppet, the Gray Puppet, Belloh-Bellah, Crub, and I were more than happy to fulfil the role of mourners at these services, but attending multiple funerals day after day, week after week, and month after month proved to be mentally and physically exhausting for us all.

Had that been the end of it, my birthday party's aftermath might not have been so tiresome. However, not long after the last of the SpaghettiOs and meatballs had been given proper burial, one of the tiny coffins buried in the Nameless Puppet's yard (one that contained a SpaghettiO) called me using a teensy tiny cell phone it had apparently taken to the grave. I have no idea how the thing got my number, but it demanded on behalf of *all* miniature coffins buried in the Nameless Puppet's yard that I dig up each and every one of them and give them all proportionately sized cell phones so that they could all call their moms to tell them they would never be coming home again for supper. I tried to explain to this coffin the sheer absurdity of this request, that none of them had moms, that the Nameless Puppet had built every last one of them in its basement, but the stubborn little thing would have none of it.

So we ordered hundreds of thousands of miniature, yet fully functional cell phones and set to work digging everything up again. And as it turned out, by some preposterous miracle, each of the coffins *did* have a mom, and these coffin-moms had been worried sick about their coffin-children and were quite grateful when their coffin-children finally called to say they would never be coming home for supper. Unfortunately for us, however, after each coffin got off the phone with its coffin-mom, it demanded a fully catered funeral service before being reburied.

After the ridiculous business with the coffins was finally taken care of, we thought it might be time for us to rest, but then those hundreds of thousands of tiny shotguns—all of which had sprouted arms, legs, eyes, and mouths of their own—demanded proper burial and funerals too, so that the Nameless Puppet (the poor thing!) had to manufacture hundreds of thousands more miniature coffins, and the rest of us were obliged to fashion hundreds of thousands more crosses and dig as many more tiny graves!

I won't even bother to tell you what those scores of insolent little cell phones demanded of us after we took care of the shotguns. You can probably guess.

Finally, after ten long years and just a week shy of my fortieth birthday, we were finished with this nonsense. The time to rest had arrived. No more digging holes, no more making coffins and crosses, no more protracted graveside funeral services (that half-mannequin, half-marionette priest could have used a lesson or two in brevity), and no more ordering flowers, food, tiny shotguns, or miniature cell phones.

Belloh-Bellah the Funtime-TERROR-Effigy had planned on resuming its world travels, but the puppet decided it might as well stay for my fortieth birthday. Crub was ninety years old now and had slowed down considerably. The two mannequins from Two Mannequins and a Truck moved into the old man's house to help take care of him (we should all be so lucky when and if we reach such a ripe old age!) But as far as playing the party planner, Crub was finished. He passed that torch on to the Nameless Puppet.

Yesterday, I detected mischief and glee in the Nameless Puppet's twinkling blue eye when it had us over for lukewarm, insipid tea and dry, crumbly little cakes. The Nameless Puppet doesn't know it, but I caught it giggle-whispering to Crub first, then to Belloh-Bellah, then to the Gray Puppet, and lastly to one of the mannequins. Consequently, I know the Nameless Puppet has something very special planned for my fortieth birthday. I'm not positive, but I could have sworn I heard the puppet whisper the words, "We're going to dig up *all* the Chicken McNuggets, SpaghettiOs, meatballs, shotguns, and cell phones!" I'm also pretty sure it whispered something to the effect of "And I've even invited all the tiny coffin-moms to the party!"

Again, I can't be absolutely certain the Nameless Puppet whispered such wondrous whimsies, but that's what it sounded like to me. Either way, I do believe my fortieth birthday party is going to be even bigger and better than my thirtieth!

At any rate, if there's one thing I'm certain of in this rotten, stinking, miserable world, it's that the Nameless Puppet does indeed put the "p" in "puppet"!!!!!!!!!!!!!!!!!!!!!!!

THE END THE END THE END THE END THE END
THE END THE END THE END THE END
THE END THE END THE END
THE END THE END
THE END

Got Me a Date with an Uptown Girl

After owning a beeper for decades and not receiving a single page on the damn thing, I concluded there must be something wrong with my beeper number. So I called my service provider to change it. As a consequence, I also had to order a new batch of social calling cards, ones that displayed my new beeper number. I placed a bulk order online, got a pretty good deal for 5,000 cards. After the weighty box arrived in the mail a few days later, I got into my car and spent the day driving around to place my cards all over town—to let people know I was out there in the world, that I existed, that I was a person in need of social interaction.

I left my calling cards on tables and chairs in the waiting rooms of doctors' offices, dental practices, psychiatry practices, and law firms. I left them on the sinks in public bathrooms—men's and ladies' rooms alike—in movie theaters, shopping malls, restaurants, and gas stations. On park benches, in bus stops, on the seats of subway cars. I tacked them to utility poles underneath garage sale fliers, above notices for missing cats and dogs. I left them strewn about on the floors and shelves of discount retail stores and supermarkets. I slipped them into the mailboxes of houses, apartments, businesses, and places of worship.

I left my calling cards all over downtown. All over midtown and uptown too. Three days it took me to get rid of them all.

Several months passed before my beeper finally went BEEP, BEEP, BEEP... I was at home in my trailer when it happened, relaxing in my recliner, playing Sega Genesis, and smoking a fat clown tear-laced primo. That my beeper had finally beeped was exciting enough, but I also noticed the number flashing on the device had an uptown area code, which was cause for even more excitement. See, in depositing my calling cards all over my city and its environs, I sought acquaintanceship, friendship, romance, meaningless sex, and anything and everything in between. But the ultimate payoff of this practice was to land a date with an uptown girl. At least that had always been the dream of *this* downtown man.

"Hello," a young woman's voice picked up when I called the number.

"Uh, hi. I'm Chester Kristofferson VIII. Did you, like, just page me?"

"Yes. Hi, I'm Juliet. I found one of your calling cards in the tomato bin at the grocery store."

"Oh. Cool. So, are you like a real uptown girl?"

"Yes, I am. I'm beautiful, blonde, rich, classy, cultured—the whole nine yards. Hey, did you just call me on your cell phone?"

"Yeah."

"Then why didn't you just put your cell phone number on your calling cards instead of your beeper number? I didn't even know what a beeper was until I googled 'beeper' after I found your card. You're probably like the last person on Earth who still uses one of those things."

"I suppose I could've put my cell number on the cards instead."

"And what's with this whole calling card thing to begin with? Who even does that? It's weird. And creepy. I mean, has anyone ever passed out social calling cards like this?"

"Uh, yeah. I mean, I think so. I think people did it back in the olden days sometimes."

"Is it still the olden days?"

"Are you always this sarcastic?"

"Yes."

"Hey, would you like to maybe…you know…go out on, like, a date with, uh, like, me sometime, maybe?"

"Pick me up at seven," Juliet said before she hung up.

***

I used up most of my life savings to rent a stretch limo for the date. Unfortunately, I was only able to afford the limo and not a driver to drive it, so I was obliged to be my own chauffeur. After I picked up the wheels, I purchased a James Bond costume from the bargain bin at a Halloween store. See, I wanted to impress Juliet by wearing a tuxedo, but I didn't even own a cheap suit, let alone a tux. I sure as shit couldn't afford to rent one after shelling out the dough for the limo. The James Bond Halloween costume was essentially a fake tuxedo. It would have to do.

Back at my trailer, I shat, showered, shaved, and doused myself in Axe body spray. On my way out the door, I grabbed a CD I'd created earlier in the day consisting solely of the song "Uptown Girl" by Billy Joel played over and over again hundreds of times.

Somewhere along the highway during the ride from downtown to uptown, with "Uptown Girl" playing at a low, comfortable volume, I realized I didn't know where the hell I was going. Juliet had never given me her address. So I called her on my cellie.

"Hello, Chester," my beeper's unmistakable, tinny, babyish voice answered on the other end.

What the fuck! I thought as my right hand fell from the steering wheel to grapple at my right hip, where my beeper should have been clipped to the elastic waistband of my fake tuxedo pants.

It wasn't.

"Where the hell are you?" I barked.

"I'm at Juliet's mansion. You know, uptown. I'm on a date with her. A fuck-first-eat-later kind of date, if you know what I mean. Heh-hch. Sorry, but I gotta go now."

"Now just you hold on a minute, you little shit. That's MY uptown girl you're with! Tell me where you are. Gimme her goddamn address. RIGHT NOW, ASSHOLE!"

"Sorry, but I'm afraid I can't do that, Chester. And by the way, I quit. Go find yourself a new beeper. Better yet, maybe it's time you catch up to the twenty-first century and stop using beepers and those ridiculous calling cards. You might want to lay off the terrible Axe body spray too."

"Why you motherfuck—"

"Don't be cross, boss. Or ex-boss, I should say. Hey, I'm not such a bad beeper. In fact, I felt kinda bad about this whole business, so after I slipped away from you earlier today, I decided to hook you up, mofo! Press the button to lower the privacy partition in your limo. Take a look in the back, and you'll see just what I mean."

Though I was bristling with rage, I pressed the button to lower the tinted sheet of glass that separated me from the passenger area. I glanced up at the rearview mirror to see a ripe corpse propped up all the way in the back. Despite the bloating and the liquefying stage of putrefaction, I recognized the body as belonging to a former neighbor of mine from the trailer park: Ol' Man Jenkins, an elderly, morbidly obese man who had somehow managed to hang himself in his trailer not two weeks prior. Now this colossal stiff was in my limo, still wrapped up in his plus-size death-suit, only now he sported a wig of long, straight, shiny platinum hair, and his thin, receding lips were all gooped up with garish, blood-red lipstick, producing a grotesque clownish effect. That enormous belly of his looked like it might burst at any second under the mounting internal pressure of the corpse gases brewing within.

"Ta-da!" my beeper said. "I made you your very own uptown girl!"

"I'm gonna find you, you obsolete little shit," I said through clenched teeth. "You hear me, you sonofabitch? And when I do, I'm gonna spike you down on the ground and stomp you into thousand bits and pieces!"

"Hey, good talk, bro, good talk. But I gotta go, yo. Juliet's about to give me an A+ uptown blowjob!" To my chagrin, I heard Juliet giggling in the background. "Sorry you don't appreciate the parting gift that took me so much trouble to prepare for you. So I guess this is see ya never again, dickface. Ah-hahahaha..."

My former beeper hung up on me.

I glanced back at the grisly thing in the backseat. Shuddering, I slapped the button to raise the tinted glass so I wouldn't have to look at it anymore. Not sure what to do next, I turned up the volume of "Uptown Girl" a few notches and just kept driving, eventually getting off the exit ramp to uptown. As I navigated the mansion-lined avenues of the uptown hills, I couldn't help but glance in the rearview mirror at that tinted glass barrier, a pit of dread ballooning in my guts. At some point the intercom beeped, startling me.

"Taaaake meeee back to the cemeteeery," Ol' Man Jenkins' croaked through the speaker. "Lower me back into my graaaaave. Then stay down there with meeeeeee. We can play *Empire Strikes Back* down there. You can be Luke Skywalker, and I'll be that tauntaun that froze to death on Hoth. You can cut open my gas-filled belly and climb inside. It will smell bad, but it'll keep you warm and protect you from the frigid Hoth niiiiiiiiiiiight!"

Fuck.

Shit.

But sadly enough, it appeared I didn't have anything better to do.

"Okay, Ol' Man Jenkins," I said, defeated. "I guess we can go play *Empire Strikes Back* in your fucking grave." I paused, sighed heavily. "Hey, you know what?"

"Whaaaaaat?" the horrifying, undead voice rasped through the intercom.

"You're my uptown girl."

"And youuuu, you are my downtown maaaaaaan."

I smiled and frowned at the exact same time, blinked away boiling hot, chimpanzee-semen tears from my crispy tater tot eyes, and took a big bite out of a Rubik's cube that I'd brought along for a snack.

"That's what I am," I said, grinding colorful plastic between my molars.

The Case of the Already-Solved Case

When Mrs. Eleanor Henderson called upon me—Douglas Hackle, Licensed Private Investigator—to solve the case of her husband's murder, the case had been closed for over three years.

On June 4, 2009, Mrs. Henderson's husband, Gregory Henderson, was killed by a chainsaw-wielding maniac named Dizzy-o Parcheezy on a busy street in downtown Dapperchild, Illinois. The victim had been on his lunch break and walking back to his office, a bag of Taco Bell in hand, when Parcheezy stepped out from an alley and decapitated the man with a chainsaw. Parcheezy proceeded to leisurely cut up the rest of Henderson's body right there on the sidewalk in broad daylight in front of hundreds of onlookers, many of whom used their cell phones to record the crime. When he was done dismembering Henderson to his satisfaction, Parcheezy strolled on over to the nearby Dapperchild First Precinct Police Station and turned himself in, confessing to the crime.

Parcheezy was convicted of first-degree murder eight months later and sentenced to life in prison, avoiding the death penalty by pleading guilty by reason of batshit insanity.

An open-and-shut case if there ever was one.

But that hadn't stopped the widow Henderson from calling me nearly four years after the fact, asking me to solve the murder.

"Um, ma'am," I'd said, trying to be polite, "you do know the killer turned himself in right after he murdered your husband, right? He was convicted and imprisoned for life."

"Yes, I know," the woman said through her sobs. "But I don't care! I want you to solve my husband's murder!"

"But, ma'am. There's, like, nothing to solve. Justice has already been served, ma'am."

"I don't care. Please find the man who killed my husband and bring him to justice! I'll pay handsomely. How does five hundred thousand smackeroonies sound to you?"

I wasn't exactly in a position where I could turn down a cool half mil. Know what I'm sayin', Sauce-Masta McDrizzle? I mean, is anyone in that position? So never mind that the gig didn't make a lick of fucking sense. I needed that money. Bad. See, I had literally hundreds of illegitimate children scattered throughout the country and hundreds of angry baby mamas sending lawyers after me to get me to cough up a king's ransom in child support every month.

So I took the case, yo.

***

I had a friend on the Dapperchild police force who agreed to pull the Henderson case file for me. I planned on examining it with my jumbo-sized private eye magnifying glass to see if I could find any clues. Only problem was I was out in the burbs, and I needed to get all the way downtown to meet him at the police station, which necessitated me driving my car. Unfortunately, the tags on my beat-up, '96 Chrysler Sebring shitbox convertible had expired. In order to renew my registration and get new tags, I was obliged to go to the E-Check station and have my car tested.

So I waited in the long line at the station for two miserable hours before finally pulling up into the building to be served.

"Please exit your vehicle, sir, and step over to the waiting area," a grumpy female inspector garbed in grease-stained coveralls said. "The test will only take a few minutes."

I did as instructed, grabbing my chainsaw from the front passenger seat before I climbed out of my car (I usually kept a chainsaw on my person as a security precaution, as I couldn't afford a proper handgun at the time, what with all that child support I was doling out every month).

The customer ahead of me—a hot dame—was sitting inside the glass-enclosed waiting area. I sat on the bench across from her, setting my chainsaw down next to me. She looked up from her *InTouch* magazine. I smiled, winked my left peeper, which happened to contain a fiber-optic implant that twinkled whenever I winked at someone, like a movie star's eye. The vixen pulled a sour face, rolled her eyes, and shook her head to indicate she was not impressed before returning her attention to her magazine.

A minute later, the inspector walked into the room, handed the woman a printout, and said, "You're all set. Your vehicle passed." Then she turned to me. "Sorry, sir. But your vehicle did not pass."

"Whaddaya mean it didn't pass?" I asked.

"Do you speak English?" she asked, all snarky and mean. "Your. Vehicle. Did. Not. Pass. We all drive Es nowadays. Your vehicle failed the E-Check because it's not an E, you moron. Oh, and by the way, your shitty car's engine just blew up."

"We all drive Es nowadays?" I asked in confusion. "What are you talking about, toots? I thought the E-Check was to test vehicle emissions."

Both dames laughed at me.

So I looked out the window. Sure enough, the "vehicle" in front of mine—the one belonging to the dame—was a big, white, three-dimensional letter E about nine feet wide and twelve feet tall. Like the plaything of a Godzilla-sized kindergartener. A ladder bolted to the side of the E led up to its roof, where a steering wheel was affixed to an exposed, slanted steering column like on a dune buggy. Also attached to the roof were two upholstered car-like seats. I glanced over to the right to see a procession of identical Es queued outside the station, all mounted by drivers who were no doubt feeling as impatient as I'd felt while waiting in that damn line.

"Oh, yeah?" I said, angry as hell as I leaned down to pull the start rope on my chainsaw. It fired up on the first pull. "Well, take this you man-hating, bra-burning, slutty, slut-shaming, feminazi SLUT!" I spun around and chopped the inspector's head clean off.

The other dame sprung up from the bench with a horrified gasp, and we both stared down at the decapitated body for a moment, watching it bleed out onto the floor.

SMACK!

The dame slapped me hard across the face.

"That highly misogynistic remark you just made offended me!" she said as she crossed her arms over the pair of luscious, grapefruit-like mounds concealed behind the tight blazer of her business suit.

"Hey, dollface, shouldn't you be a little more offended by the fact that I just chopped somebody's fucking head off?"

"Kiss me, you fool," she blurted unexpectedly as she leaned in and smashed her lips against mine, one of her legs kicking back so her high-heeled foot hung suspended in midair as we smooched, just like in the movies.

***

The inspector was right—my rust bucket had finally broken down for good. So the dame offered me a ride downtown.

We climbed the ladder on her E. She plopped down in the driver seat, I in the passenger seat. I'd never ridden on an E before. The thing didn't appear to have wheels. It just sort of glided along the road like a sled. Everywhere around us people were driving identical Es. During the drive downtown, I did not spot a single car, truck, bus, or train.

Call me unobservant, but for whatever reason, I had somehow failed to notice the apparent wholesale shift in transportation from automobiles to Es that had occurred at some point in the past. See, each of us has our own unique frame of reference. In our separate paths in life, we all come to learn or not learn completely different facts, truths, and bits of misinformation. But, goddamnit, if someone thinks it's funny or pathetic that I missed this whole E thing, that someone can just say so to my fucking face, and that someone will find himself French kissing the buzzing blade of my goddamn, motherfucking 17.3-horsepower Leatherface special, goddamn it!

At any rate, it occurred to me during the ride that I didn't need to see the Henderson case file. I already knew who the killer was. I also knew exactly where to find him. So I had the skirt drop me off at the nearby state penitentiary instead of the police station. She pulled up next to the towering barbed wire fence that girded the prison grounds, then demanded that I have sex with her as payment for the ride. We did the deed right there on top of the E.

Which turned out to be a big mistake, as I was to find out later that I impregnated her that day—and with quintuplets no less! Identical ones too. Five boys who looked exactly like me. Yup, that's another five little Douglas Hackles crawling around on this miserable rock we call Earth, each of whom will undoubtedly grow up to be a blithering douchecanoe asshole just like their old man. And in the meantime, that's another hefty child support check for me to shell out every month, goddamn it!

Anyhow, as I mounted the ladder to disembark the E, the dame called out, "Please don't go! I love you, Douglas Hackle!!!"

I paused for a second, turned to her and said, "Pfft. You don't love me. You just love my Douggie-Style," and resumed my climb down.

After the dame glided away on her E, crying her eyes out, I pulled out my magnifying glass and used it to concentrate the sun's rays on the fence, just like I used to do to ants and leaves when I was a kid. Within minutes, I'd burned a hole big enough to climb through. Then I tried the magnifying glass trick on the reinforced concrete wall of the prison, to great success. Before long, I'd breached the four-foot-thick barrier and was inside the Big House. Using my chainsaw to take out any sucka-ass prison guards unlucky enough to get in my way, I pushed deeper and deeper into the cellblocks in search of Dizzy-o Parcheezy until eventually I found his skinny, batshit-crazy ass jerking off in his cell.

I busted him out and delivered him forthwith to the 1st Precinct, where I triumphantly informed the police I'd captured the notorious Dizzy-o Parcheezy, cold-blooded murderer of Gregory Henderson, and they could now finally bring the man to justice.

As you may well imagine, the cops dragged both of us away.

I used my one phone call to inform the widow Henderson that I had solved the already-solved case.

Not a year later, I was tried and convicted for multiple chainsaw murders, breaking a convicted murderer out of prison, failure to make my child support payments, slut-shaming, slut-shaming-shaming (the crime of shaming slut-shamers), misogyny, misandry, misanthropy, anvil-shaming, chair-shaming, paperclip-shaming, burning ants with a magnifying glass when I was a kid, and a host of other infractions of the law. I pled guilty to all counts by reason of batshit insanity and received twenty consecutive life sentences in a federal maximum security prison.

Another open-and-shut case if there ever was one.

Nevertheless, I still hired Dizzy-o Parcheezy (he was released from prison on parole a few months ago and now works as a licensed P.I.) to figure out who the hell broke him out of jail and to find out if Douglas Hackle is even still alive. Word in the slammer is that Parcheezy has a bigger magnifying glass than mine and a bigger cock to boot. If he solves the case, I promised I'd give him the half million dollars I earned from the Henderson case, but he said all he wants in return for solving the case is a chance to surf the tops of palm trees in a Model T Ford driven by a hardscrabble vagabond with a foretaste for mythopoetic, snappish, sentient anvils held in thrall of a Prussian-Arabian fetal polar bear in the pink of health via a Kierkegaardian karate class-warfare unwitnessed by the unsung, fretful fugue-frogs of protean pear-bears par excellence thwarting the seventeen ontological tip-taps of post-*Krull*, pre-Ratt Malay$ia-Kentucky if by the sdfdjasklfjdskl-ajfasfskdlajfklsjdafkljdsaklfdsklafyrewuiklsdajfklds.ak?/lfjdask lfs[am+kljsa?klf jdskl ajfklsjdafklfdsafdsklafjdlsafjs7Q2;kdlajfd !lsajfld8af3saf2sdlsiorjn3e9u5t243t89 Q=GB{d&*(24 umv89h jwi9ogijfeowgjwegiorje%^&*etrklpsdfdsafdsa&*(@$#?$?$ $3 45 ert435rt3e 4rf4r5 t y45 6retyuertyju3e4tyru43rte2

Flawless Face®

On the morning of Larry Perkins' twelve-year anniversary of employment with F.F. Incorporated, the company's VP of Operations, Jack Hartindale, paid him a visit.

"Morning, Larry," the VP said at the threshold of Larry's cubicle.

"Hey, Jack. What's up?"

"I'm afraid I'm going to have to let you go, Larry."

"Let me go? Whaddaya mean?"

"You're fired, Larry."

"But...but, why? I've been the sales manager here at F.F.'s New York branch for twelve years now. Under my watch, a quarter hasn't gone by where we haven't met or exceeded our sales quota."

"Do you know what at-will employment means, Larry?"

"Of course."

"At-will employment means I can fire you without reason. However, since you want to know, I'll tell you why I fired you: I don't like the way you look, Larry."

Larry was taken aback. "What are you even talking about, Jack? There's nothing wrong with the way I look. I've never once violated dress code and my personal grooming is impeccable."

"Your personal grooming is impeccable, Larry. That's not what this is about. The problem is I don't like your fucking face, Larry."

"Wh-what? What's wrong with my face?"

"Again, by law, Larry, I owe you no explanation. But since you asked, I suspect it might be something about the definition of your cheekbones, or perhaps the curve of your jawline, or maybe even the jut of your nose. I can't quite put a finger on it myself. Anyway, it doesn't fucking matter. I don't like your face, and since I don't like your face, you're fucking fired. I'll give you about fifteen minutes to clear your workstation. Then, before you leave the building for the last time, I'll come back and take you around to introduce you to everyone in the office."

After Jack sauntered off, Larry sat in his chair for a minute processing the news, a look of bewilderment plastered to his face as he ran his fingers lightly over his cheekbones, jawline, and nose. Eventually, he stood up and walked in a daze to the office supplies closet, where he grabbed a box to pack his things.

As promised, Jack returned fifteen minutes later to take Larry around the office and introduce him to everybody. Jack started by introducing himself to Larry.

"Hello. I'm Jack Hartindale, VP of Operations here at F.F." He extended a hand to Larry. Larry took Jack's hand in his, and the two men shook firmly.

"Hi, I'm Larry Per—"

"Let's move on now, shall we?"

Larry followed Jack a few steps over to the cubicle that adjoined his own.

"Dan?" Jack said as he knocked on the metallic edge of the cube. Dan Parker, Sales Team Leader, spun around to face Jack and Larry. "Dan, this is Larry Perkins. Larry was the Sales Manager of your branch. He was your boss. I fired him today."

"It's great to finally meet you after all these years," Dan said, smiling good-naturedly.

Larry and Dan shook hands. "It's great to finally meet you too," Larry said. "Seems like it was just yesterday when I interviewed and hired you. When was that, five years ago?"

"Yeah, five years next month," Dan said. "Time certainly does fly. Well, sorry to see you go, Larry."

"Thanks. You take care."

"You too."

Larry and Jack continued moving down the row of cubicles. The next one belonged to Erin Morris, a sales associate.

"Erin, this is Larry Perkins," Jack said. "Larry was the sales manager of your branch. He was your boss. I fired him today."

"It's so nice to finally meet you," Erin said, proffering a hand.

"Likewise," Larry said, shaking the young woman's hand. "You're one of our best sales associates, Erin. It's been a pleasure working with you, and I have no doubt you'll go far in the company."

"Aw, that's so nice of you to say! Let me return the compliment by saying you're one of the best bosses I've ever had. In fact, and not to be impertinent, but I can't imagine why they'd fire you."

"It's my face."

"Your face? What's wrong with your face?"

"I don't know," Larry said. "Ask him." He jabbed a thumb at the VP.

Erin eyed the VP's unsmiling face, taking the hint not to inquire any further about the subject. She nervously chuckled instead, if only to break the awkward silence.

"What's wrong is I don't like the way it looks," Jack said.

"Oh...of course," Erin said. "Well, sorry to see you go, Larry. Good luck."

"Good luck to you too," Larry said.

Thirty people were employed at F.F.'s NYC branch office, and that morning Jack took Larry around to meet each one of them for the first time, though Larry already knew them well, having worked with most of them for years.

He'd just never met any of them.

"Before you leave us today," Jack said back at Larry's cube, "let me ask you this: Have you ever wondered what it is you and your team having been selling all these years here at F.F. Incorporated?"

"No, I haven't."

"F.F. makes one product," Jack said. He held out a plain white box about the size of phonebook in one hand. With his free hand, Jack removed the lid from the box. Inside was a mask fashioned from a transparent gel-like substance. But for the eyeholes, nose holes, and mouth hole, the mask was featureless.

"This is what you've been selling for the last twelve years, Larry. We call it the Flawless Face®. That's what the two F's in F.F. Incorporated stand for, by the way. When worn, a

Flawless Face® will mold itself to the wearer's face in such a way that the person's face will appear likeable and attractive to everyone in the world no matter how unlikeable or unattractive that person's real face is. The product was specifically developed to prevent bosses from firing their employees simply because they didn't like the way their faces looked. Also, any individual who has *already* been fired because their boss didn't like the way their face looked can usually get their old job back simply by putting on a Flawless Face® and showing their former boss that they now wear one. This one I'm holding here is for you, Larry. Compliments of the company. Please accept it as parting gift from F.F. Incorporated for your many years of service. Again, Larry, just in case I wasn't clear, I can virtually guarantee that I'd give you job back if you put this Flawless Face® on right now."

Larry took the box from the VP. "Thank you," he said.

The two men stood facing one another for one last protracted, awkward moment, Larry staring down at the Flawless Face® but not taking any sort of action.

"Well, so long, Larry. Please exit the building now or I'll be forced to call security."

***

The economy was shit, so Larry never found another job. A month after getting fired from F.F. Incorporated, he was evicted from his apartment. He was starving and had nowhere to go. But those were the least of Larry's problems. See, it was not a good time to be homeless in NYC. Every evening at nightfall, scores of bloodthirsty TERROR PUPPETS came out of the shadows to prey upon anyone out past curfew.

Larry didn't last one night on the streets. When those ferocious little abominations of nature finally caught him, cornering him at the back of an alley, he clutched his Flawless Face® to his chest.

"If only I could have figured out a way to get my fucking job back!" Larry cried moments before the TERROR DOLLS pounced on him.

"Hey, wait…shit! How could I have been so damn stupid? All I had to do was…"

But it was too late. As an act of desperation, the doomed man quickly stretched the Flawless Face® over his flawed face in the hope that it might ward off the TERROR DOLLS. Unfortunately, those masks were not designed for such purposes, and the TERROR DOLLS rent Larry down to a stinking pile of blood, guts, muscle, bone, fat, sinew, skin, hair, shit, bile, lymph, chyme, chyle, shit, piss, semen, tears, and shredded bits of a Flawless Face®.

***

Moral of the story: Don't be a dumbass, son!

The Bored Ouija Board

"My latest problem," the Ouija board said as it eased back into the therapist's couch to get more comfy, "is that I'm bored."

"Bored?" the therapist asked. "Bored of what?"

"Bored of being a Ouija board, I guess. See, Doc, a good deal of my life has been spent rotting on the shelves of thrift stores in podunk towns in flyover states across the country, usually sandwiched between a couple of old, musty board games—Monopoly, Chutes and Ladders, Clue, and the like. And when I'm not rotting on a shelf in a thrift store, I'm usually collecting dust in someone's hallway closet, someone who bought me for a degrading fifty cents or less, where I find myself once again sandwiched between old board games, only now I'm enveloped in complete darkness. On occasion, my owner might take me out during a party, wherein drunken assholes ask me stupid questions and maneuver the planchette themselves in an attempt to scare each other or stir up some laughter by spelling out ridiculous or obscene phrases. Eventually, I'm either sold back to another thrift store or else given away at a garage sale for fucking pennies, the vicious cycle of my so-called life beginning anew.

"Yeah, sure, occasionally people buy me who believe in my power, people who use me to communicate with the spirit world. And it used to be that whenever I fell into the hands of such an owner, I was ecstatic with joy. How I loved when people took me seriously. When these folks used me to contact their dead loved ones, it made me feel important, made me feel like I belonged in the world. After all, that's the purpose for which I was made. But now, even that has lost its charm. See, you can only help so many people connect with their dead spouses or grandmas before it starts getting old. Nowadays, helping people talk to the dead just doesn't give me the sense of fulfillment it used to. I mean, I don't want to feel this way. I wish I could get my old verve back. But it's been years since I felt any sort of enthusiasm for my existence. Like I said, Doc. I'm just bored of being a Ouija board."

"Has it ever occurred to you," the therapist said in a somewhat condescending, mister-know-it-all sort of tone, "that perhaps your boredom stems from the fact that you might possibly be the biggest fucking asshole ever to walk the face of this planet?"

The Ouija board was taken aback for moment, its invisible tongue tied. "Um, no, that has never occurred to me, Doc. I mean, as far as sentient Ouija boards go, I think I'm a pretty nice guy. What are you trying to insinuate?"

"Oh, I'm not trying to insinuate anything. I was just throwing that out there, is all. Just something to think about. Let's move on now, shall we?"

"Wait. Just something to think about? But why would I want to think about something that isn't in the least bit true. And why would you even say that to me? Why would you—"

"Let's move on now, shall we? So when you called me to set up our appointment, you also mentioned you were having problems with anxiety."

"Um, yeah. Yeah, I am. Like I was saying, I'm usually never in one place for more than a few years, maybe a decade at the most. So I constantly worry that as soon as I start to feel comfortable in, for example, a particularly cozy closet or on an especially nice, well-kept shelf in a junk store, I'll be sold off and shipped out the next day without warning. Not only that, but my lost sense of purpose, identity, and self-worth has sent my anxiety levels through the roof, too. I also started a new job about a month ago. A real job. It's my first job ever, and—"

"Has it ever occurred to you," the therapist interrupted, "that perhaps—and again I stress the word *perhaps*—your anxiety is actually caused by the fact that you might be a blithering, insufferable, raging asshole of the most epic proportions ever imagined?"

"Hey, I'm *not* an asshole! Why do you keep suggesting that? Why, I oughta leave right—"

"Relax, my friend, relax. I was just throwing that out there, is all. Just something to think about. Nothing more. Anyways, let's move on, shall we? You also mentioned that you're suffering from severe clinical depression. Let's talk a little bit about that."

The flustered Ouija board composed himself before he continued. "Well, yes. The primary cause of my depression, as I told you over the phone, is the recent and tragic loss of my entire family."

"You didn't go into much detail about it over the phone, which is perfectly understandable. Why don't you tell me more about it now? Remember, I'm your therapist. You can tell me anything, no matter how difficult something is to talk about. Doing so will be therapeutic for you."

The Ouija board sighed. "Okay. To make a long story short, I met a female Ouija board about two years ago at Foo-Fap's Thrift-World Emporium in Dapperboy, Illinois, where we were both sitting on the board game shelf awaiting new buyers. It was love at first sight. At our request, a sentient cassock—you know, those long garments that priests wear—that happened to be hanging in the nearby Miscellaneous Apparel section married us right there on our shelf. That first year, my wonderful wife bore me two children: two little Ouija boards—a boy and a girl—each of them no bigger than a playing card. Our little family enjoyed a short but happy few months in the thrift store, before a nice, young newlywed couple came in and purchased us. We were thankful beyond words that the couple chose to buy all four of us, when they could have just as easily broken our family apart.

"All was perfect until that horrible, twisted, multiple-vehicle pile-up that happened on the interstate on the way from the thrift store to our new owners' house that day. We...we never did get a chance to see our new home. I...I was the sole survivor of the car crash." The Ouija board paused before crying out, "And cursed be the day that I was mass produced at a Parker Brothers toy factory in China by malnourished, blinded, hobbled, two-year-old slave laborers!" He lapsed into silence again, overcome by emotion. "That crash," he resumed, "it happened not three months ago. So as you can see, Doc, the root cause of my severe clinical depression is quite obvi—"

"Has the possibility ever occurred to you," the therapist interrupted, "that the *real* reason you're experiencing severe clinical depression is that, of all the self-centered, blithering, raging, drooling, narcissistic, douche-canoeing assholes that have ever stumbled across the face of this goddamn, miserable, motherfucking planet, that you are without a doubt the most insufferable, inconceivable, unbearable, insupportable, unbelievable, outrageous, and astonishing fucking asshole to ever exist *anywhere* in the whole motherfucking, cock-sucking, shit-eating universe!?!?"

"That's it," the Ouija board said as he hopped down from the couch to the floor. "I don't have to take this kind of abuse from you. I'll find myself another therapist, one who isn't batshit-crazier than me. You're a quack and a disgrace to your profession. And you're not even a human. Shit, you're not even a sentient Ouija board! As a matter of fact, I'm staring at you right now, and I still have no idea what the fuck you are. But you know what, pal? I don't care what you are. Because you, sir, are no longer a part of my life. I gotta go. I'm almost late for work. So long, asshole."

The Ouija board turned from the therapist and began hopping for the door.

"Do you really want to know what I am?" the therapist called after him.

The Ouija board halted just before the exit, waited for the therapist to continue, though he refused to look back.

"I'll tell you what I am," said the therapist. "Here goes. You know how if Suri Cruise were to put on a cheap, plastic Brad Pitt mask just before using a chainsaw to chop off everyone's head in the world whose name began with the letter "Q", that would not change the fact that, in the video game Frogger, if you land your frog on the back of a diving turtle and sit there for too long, you'll die because the diving turtles eventually dive back under the water?"

"What? You lost me there."

"I'll repeat myself then. You how if Suri Cruise were to put on a cheap, plastic Brad Pitt mask just before..." the therapist said, repeating the entire sentence.

"Um, yeah," the Ouija board said after hearing it a second time. "I guess so. I mean, that's a completely ridiculous, stupid, and pointless thing to observe, but I suppose it's true."

"Well, *that* is what I am."

"What? That makes no sense. Are you saying that you're some kind of physical incarnation of that absurd fact?"

"Indeed, that's exactly what I'm saying. Turn around and look at me, and you shall see."

The Ouija board, who was still facing the door, turned to look at the therapist, who was on the other side of the room in front of his desk, hovering just above the carpet: a scrambled blur of shifting images, including a chainsaw-wielding Suri Cruise in a cheap Brad Pitt mask, blood-spattering decapitations, rapidly changing screenshots of the original Frogger video game, and a cyclone of scrolling, wheeling, dancing names, all beginning with the letter "Q"—*Quincy, Quentin, Quimby, Quin, Quill, Qasim, Quetzalxochitl...*

After a moment, the Ouija board said, "Wow. I hadn't noticed before. I'm sorry I doubted you. You really are the fact that if Suri Cruise were to put on a cheap, plastic Brad Pitt mask just before using a chainsaw to chop everyone's head off in the world whose name began with the letter "Q", that would not change the fact that, in the video game Frogger, if you land your frog on the back of a diving turtle and sit there for too long, you'll die because the diving turtle will eventually dive under the water."

"You're goddamn right that's what I am! Now get the fuck out of my office and never come back!"

"I was already on my way out, dick! Fuck you too!"

***

The Ouija board used his short telekinetic reach to open the door and let himself out into the hallway. He had to get to work. Luckily, he didn't have very far to go. In fact, the Ouija board worked directly across the hall from his therapist. His place of employment was only two hops away.

See, the Ouija board was a licensed psychologist too.

"Good morning, Sheila," he said to his receptionist as he hopped into the waiting room of his office, letting the door shut behind him.

"Good morning, sir," Sheila said from her desk, not bothering to look up as she finished painting her left pinkie nail a sassy-hot pink. "Your nine o'clock, Eileen Taylor, just called to cancel."

"Oh, swell. Hey, did you get the note I left for you on Friday about buying me a shotgun and a normal, inanimate Ouija board?"

"I picked them both up for you on Saturday. They're on your desk."

"Oh, splendid. I really don't know what I'd do without you, Sheila."

Sheila blew on the still wet nail polish of her outstretched fingers, looked up, smiled, and winked coquettishly at her boss.

"Who am I seeing at ten?" he asked.

The receptionist leaned in toward her monitor. "Your ten o'clock is a new patient. No name shown here. Just a description."

"A description?"

"Yeah. It says here that your ten o'clock patient is the fact that if Suri Cruise were to put on a cheap, plastic Wesley Snipes mask just before using a chainsaw to chop off everyone's head in the world whose name begins with the letter "Q", that would not change the fact that, in the video game Frogger, if you land your frog on the back of a diving turtle and sit there for too long, you'll die because the diving turtle will eventually go back under water."

The Ouija board froze in place just outside his office door. "Are you certain it says a Wesley Snipes mask and not a Brad Pitt mask?" he asked.

"Positive," she responded.

"Whew!" the Ouija board said, the interjection surfing on a long sigh of relief. "Well, that's one good thing. Hey, I'm gonna go into my office now, jump on the internet, put on some Ouija board porn, lube up my planchette, and jerk off until the damn thing breaks in half. Then I'm gonna take that shotgun you got me and blow my fucking Ouija board brains out."

Sheila gasped, raised her fingertips to her lips. "But, sir. What about your patients? Should I cancel your appointments for today. Should I, er, cancel your appointments for...*forever*?"

"Oh, no. I have every intention of keeping my appointments. That's why I had you pick up that normal, inanimate Ouija board. When my patients arrive, send them to my office just as you would normally. Only now be sure to inform them that they have to use the Ouija board that's on my desk to contact me from beyond the grave so that we can conduct our therapy sessions remotely. Got it?"

"Got it, boss!"

TERROR THING

"I'll take a Happy Meal," Silas Amadeus Cruthers XVII said to the lanky, pimply-faced teenage boy working the only open register at the only McDonald's in the town of Dapperboy, Illinois.

"Do you want that with a cheeseburger, hamburger, or Chicken McNuggets?"

"None of those. I want a Happy Meal box filled to the brim with pink slime, please. Ya know what I'm talkin' about, right, sonny? That pink slime you put in your burgers?"

"Yeah, I know. That's a special order. Costs a dollar more than a regular Happy Meal. Is that alright?"

"A dollar more!" The eighty-five-year-old cheapskate multibillionaire's face screwed itself into a gnarled scowl as his liver-spotted left hand clenched into a fist of trembling rage. After a moment, he grudgingly muttered, "Oh, alright then."

The miserable cashier stared down blankly at the register and rapidly tapped the touchscreen with two index fingers. "Do you want fries or apple slices?"

"Neither."

"What would you like to drink?"

"Nothing. I just want a Happy Meal box filled with pink slime, please. Oh, and the toy too."

"Is this for a girl or boy?"

"It's for me. What toys do you have for boys?"

"My Little Hospice toys."

"What are those like?"

The annoyed employee jabbed a thumb at the display board at the end of the counter. "My Little Hospice® - Collect All Four!" was written at the top of the board in a large, grim-looking font. Four toy hospices were attached to the board below the message, each about the size of a bar of soap. Except for their colors, the toy hospices were identical in shape and design.

Black, gray, light gray, and dark gray were the four available colors.

The old man sneered and drooled a tad. "You mean you don't have My Little Assisted Living Center toys anymore?"

The cashier rolled his eyes. "No, sir. We switched from My Little Assisted Living Center to My Little Hospice toys just this week."

"What toys do you have for girls?"

"All we have left is Elsa from *Frozen*."

"Okay, I guess I'll take one of those then."

"For here or to go, sir?"

"Pardon me, sonny. My hearing's not so good these days. 'Mind repeating that for me?" Old Man Silas leaned in, cocked his head a little, and raised a cupped hand to his ear.

"DO YOU WANT THIS FOR HERE OR TO GO, SIR!"

The old man recoiled, startled. "Well, you don't have to shout! I said I was hard of hearing, not stone deaf!" To get revenge, Old Man Silas leaned in close to the teenager and yelled, "I WANT IT TO GO!"

Shrinking away from the man's spray of spittle and foul breath, the cashier tapped the touchscreen a few more times and said, "That'll be four dollars and twenty-seven cents."

With his left hand, Old Man Cruthers reached into the breast pocket of his tailored, Italian power suit, from which he extracted his faded, ripped, creased, dog-eared Blockbuster Video card. He offered it to the cashier (in his right hand, the old man gripped an idling chainsaw, the tip of its vibrating blade nearly kissing the floor).

Staring at Old Man Cruthers like the dude was completely batshit, the cashier said, "Um, mister, that's like a Blockbuster Video card."

"I know what it is. I'm using it to pay for my Happy Meal."

"Sir, I'm not sure if you know this or not, but Blockbuster Video has been out of business for years now. And even if Blockbuster were still in business, you couldn't use that card here. This is McDonald's, sir. Those cards were used for renting movies. Renting movies at, um, like, Blockbuster Video. And even if you were renting a movie at Blockbuster, you'd still have to pay for it with cash or a credit card. Blockbuster Video cards were never used as credit cards."

"If I didn't know any better, young feller, I'd say you were talkin' back to me."

"No, sir. It's just that I can't take that card as payment. I—"

"You *are* talkin' back to me. Dang youngins these days, always disrespectin' their elders." The old man quickly pocketed his Blockbuster card and said, "Take this, punk!" He hoisted the chainsaw like fucking Leatherface, punched the throttle, and leaned over the counter to lop off the cashier's stunned head in one clean, buzzing slash.

The whole thing was completely fucked.

BLOOD! BLOOD! BLOOD! BLOOD! BLOOD! BLOOD! BLOOD! BLOOD! BLOOD! BLOOD! BLOOD!

***

Minutes later at the Taco Bell directly across the street, it was pretty much the same scene.

"Can I take your order, sir?" a plucky teenage girl said to the old man, her wet, bracey smile gleaming brightly like the gilded American Dream itself.

"I'll take ten soft tacos, please."

"Regular or supreme?"

"I want ten soft tacos filled with McDonald's pink slime. No meat or lettuce or cheese or sour cream or anything. Just the pink slime, please."

The girl's bright smile deflated into a flat line. "Um, sir, this is Taco Bell. I'm sorry, but we don't serve McDonald's pink slime here."

"Yes, I think I'll take ten soft tacos filled with McDonald's pink slime, please," the smiling, drooling old man said as if he hadn't heard the girl (and perhaps he hadn't). "And I'd like to pay with this." For the tenth time that day, Old Man Cruthers brandished his Blockbuster Video card and presented it to a cashier at a fast food restaurant in the town of Dapperboy.

And for the tenth time that day, a fast food cashier had to explain to the octogenarian why his Blockbuster Video card was a completely unacceptable form of payment.

And for the tenth time that day, a fast food cashier lost his or her pretty little head (hers, in this case) for talking back to my fuckin' boy, motherfuckin' Silas Amadeus Cruthers the goddamned 17th!!!!!!!!!!!!!!!!!!!!!!!!!!!!!!!!!!!

Wendy's, Burger King, Long John Silver's, Arby's, White Castle, Five Guys, KFC, Chick-fil-A, McDonald's, and now Taco Bell. Ten fast food joints, ten heads rolling on the goddamn floor. That's exactly how long it took the Dapperboy po-po to finally catch up to my main man.

"Freeze, asshole!" a SWAT officer who was ripped like Wesley Snipes in *Blade* shouted as Old Man Cruthers casually stepped out onto the Taco Bell parking lot. "Drop the fucking chainsaw!"

The old man halted. A SWAT team and a wall of armored vehicles surrounded him, scores of sniper rifles, assault rifles, and shotguns aimed squarely at his sunken, skull-like face. Dozens of glowing red points of light from the sniper laser sights dotted his wrinkled forehead like a living, moving fiber-optic rash.

"Don't shoot!" he said, though he did not drop the chainsaw as ordered. "I'm going to reach into my breast pocket, nice n' easy like, see? But only to grab my Blockbuster Video card so I can show it to you guys, okay? Nice n' easy like, see?"

"Don't even think about it, gramps," the lead officer said. He knelt on one knee, his SIG Sauer P220 drawn steadily, one eye clenched shut and one eye slitted to draw a perfect bead on the old man's prominent cock bulge. "And why the fuck would we want to see your goddamn Blockbuster Video card?" he asked without taking his aim off the target.

"Because if I show it to you, it will pardon me of the crimes I have committed today."

"Oh, no, it won't."

"Oh, yes, it will."

"Oh, no, it won't."

"Oh, yes, it will."

"Listen, I'm not fuckin' around with you anymore, Cruthers. No one gives a cockroach's swingin' blue nutsack about your goddamn Blockbuster Video card. Your Blockbuster Video card is a big piece of white dog shit, okay? And you're loonier than a bat fried in its own batshit, you senile, retarded child murderer. You listening to me now, asshole? Don't you even *think* about reaching in your jacket for *anything*! Drop that fuckin' chainsaw *RIGHT ... FUCKING ... NOW!*"

"Yo, fahk you, mang!" Old Man Cruthers said in his best imitation of Scarface as he dropped his right shoulder into a heaving position before locking the throttle of his chainsaw (the throttle lock was the old man's own modification). "If I'm going down, I'm takin' one of you doughnut-eatin' pig fuckers with me!" he yelled over the screaming buzz of the smoke-spewing saw.

Countless bullets slammed into the old man's gaunt body, virtually shredding him to pieces, but not before my dude got that chainsaw toss off. The thing wheeled through the air in *Matrix*-like slowmo, sailing over the incoming barrage of bullets, before splitting the lead officer's head right down the middle.

The whole thing was completely fucked.
BLOOD! BLOOD! BLOOD! BLOOD! BLOOD! BLOOD! BLOOD! BLOOD! BLOOD! BLOOD! BLOOD! BLOOD!

***

A little over two months later....

A 911 operator answered a late afternoon call: "911. Please state the nature of your emergency."

"It's my grandpa!" a little girl's peanut voice shrilled on the other end of the line. "I think he's dead!"

"Now calm down there, honey. What happened? Is your grandpa injured? Is he breathing? Why do you say he's dead?"

"Because I'm standing at the foot of his grave right now. His funeral was two months ago!"

"Hm, I see. Okay, looks like we've pinpointed your location. An ambulance is on its way to the cemetery you're at. Just stay on the line with me until help arrives, okay, sweetie? What's your name?"

"My name is Courtney Cute. I'm the cutest child in the world. Humph!"

"Okay, Courtney Cute. What is your grandpa's name?"

"Silas Amadeus Cruthers the Seventeenth." Then, bored to tears by possibly the dullest conversation she'd ever had the displeasure to participate in, the girl hung up on the operator.

Bathed in the reddening light of the setting sun, Courtney Cute stood at the foot of her grandpa's grave, clutching her doll to her chest. It was true: The girl was the cutest kid in the world. With dark brown pigtails, big sparkling blue eyes, long curved eyelashes, a button nose, rosebud lips, and chubby apple-like cheeks, she was so cute that many people died immediately upon setting eyes on her when the child's mega-cuteness caused them to go into seizures, crumble, melt, implode, or explode.

In sharp contrast, the girl's doll was the most terrifying thing on Earth, far too terrifying for me to attempt any sort of meaningful description of it here. Sure, I could say it was an unholy, primordial abomination, a thing older than the universe itself, a thing characterized by the most singularly horrific amalgamation of physical features, features that simultaneously suggested an antique Raggedy Ann doll, a malevolent dwarf-clown, a voodoo fetish doll stuffed with dogshit, a demonically possessed marionette, an aborted fetal warthog, and the charred-up corpse of a deformed baby chimpanzee. But that description would not come close to doing the thing justice.

The doll's name was TERROR THING and, with very few exceptions, anyone who'd ever laid eyes upon TERROR THING had died instantly from TERROR.

Bored out of her gourd, Courtney Cute took out her cell phone again, opened Twitter, and tweeted a single comma before putting the phone back in her pocket. Of the girl's billions of Twitter followers, hundreds were so overtaken with the mind-boggling cuteness of the girl's tweeted comma that they bled from their eyes, ears, and noses right after viewing the tweet, their heads exploding like *Scanners* seconds later. Such was the cuteness of Courtney Cute.

Old Man Cruthers' tombstone—a towering, phallic obelisk of the finest polished green-black marble—was the largest grave marker in the small Dapperboy cemetery. The inscription at the monolith's base read:

> Silas Amadeus Cruthers XVII
> Multibillionaire
> 1929 – 2015
> He was better than you
> FUCK YOU!

Notwithstanding the aforementioned overabundance of fast food restaurants in the burgh of Dapperboy, the town was quite small, so small in fact that it had only one family practice doctor, a man who also served as the town's sole ER doctor, psychiatrist, psychologist, dentist, social worker, physical therapist, chiropractor, EMT, and ambulance driver. The same man also acted as the town coroner, priest, rabbi, funeral director, embalmer, and grave digger. His name was Dr. David Dorito.

Not that it matters, but Dr. Dorito was devilishly handsome and nabbed all sorts of ass. In fact, you can't even begin to imagine how much ass this dude got. You think firemen and boy bands get mad ass? Pfft! Lemme tell you, this Dr. Dorito, he got so much fine, top-shelf, drop dead gorgeous, prom queen-grade ass that he didn't even know what to do with it! What I mean to say is that this dude got so much cream of the crop, supermodel-grade, Victoria's Secret model-quality, NFL cheerleader-caliber ass that he literally had to turn it down at his front door!

Anyway, ten minutes after the 911 call was placed, Dr. Dorito's ambulance came speeding up the cemetery drive, flashers flashing and siren screaming. After the vehicle came to a screeching stop not too far from Old Man Cruthers' grave, Dr. Dorito hopped out and ran over to Courtney Cute. As he approached, the girl concealed TERROR THING in the folds of her flowery dress so as not to scare the man to death.

"Hi there, Courtney Cute. What happened?"

"It's my grandpa! He's in a coffin. In this grave here. I think he's dead!"

"I see. Well, Courtney, I was your grandpa's doctor, dentist, chiropractor, and psychiatrist. I also performed the inquest on what was left of his unmistakably, unquestionably dead body. I even presided over his funeral service. What's more, I dug and filled in his grave by myself. I'm sorry, kiddo, but I'm afraid there's just nothing more we can do for your grandpa at this point."

"Do something, you incompetent cokehead, pedophile quack! Do something right now or I'll call 911 and tell them you tried to kidnap, rape, murder, and eat me!"

"Okay, okay! Calm down, little poppet. Let me see what I can do."

The good doctor grabbed a shovel leaning on a nearby tombstone, the same shovel he'd used to bury the old man two months ago. After about an hour of digging, he struck the lid of the coffin. A couple minutes later, Dr. Dorito pried open the lid to reveal the ghastly remains of Old Man Cruthers.

If you recall, my dude had taken like four hundred bullets from head to toe. So as you can well imagine, Old Man Cruthers hadn't looked all that great the day they'd planted him in the dirt. Two months of decomposition hadn't done much to improve my main man's overall appearance either. But Dr.

Dorito had a strong stomach and was not at all put off by the putrid, liquefying horror inside that coffin.

"Hmm," he intoned from his hunched position in the grave. "I don't think this is as bad as it looks, actually. A few Band-Aids might do the trick." He reached into his medical bag and took out a handful of decorative Band-Aids, including Scooby-Doo, SpongeBob, Spider-Man, Hello Kitty, Strawberry Shortcake, Dora the Explorer, My Little Pony, My Little Assisted Living Center, My Little Hospice, My Little Funeral Parlor, and My Little Crematorium Band-Aids. Quickly removing the plastic cover strips, he placed dozens of Band-Aids onto the greasy, black, pulpy lump that was all that remained of Old Man Cruthers' head. Then he stuck Band-Aids all over the tailored $1.4 million Italian death suit that concealed the corpse's ruined torso and limbs.

After placing a My Little Fourth Late Term Abortion Band-Aid on one of Old Man Cruthers' shiny black ten thousand dollar shoes, Dr. Dorito grabbed his medical bag and climbed out of the grave.

"Your grandpa should come through any moment now," he said, smiling as he gave the girl two light pats on the head.

And he was right! The dripping, moaning, reanimated husk of Old Man Cruthers sat up in the coffin mere seconds later.

"Grandpa!" Courtney Cute squealed.

"Oooooh, marrr aaarr dahhhh oooo aaaaaaaaaa!" the corpse blubbered, holding its head-lump with both its greasy, black, skeletal hands as if it had merely woken up to a bad hangover headache. After a moment, it managed to crawl out of the grave, stand up, and hug its beaming granddaughter.

"Glad to see you're back on your feet, Mr. Cruthers," Dr. Dorito said, smiling that big megawatt smile of his. "Well, I should really get going now. The usual crowd of stunningly beautiful, absurdly hot, Miss America-grade ass is congregating out on my front lawn as we speak, and I really should get back home and try to satisfy at least a dozen of them before I go to bed. But before I do, can I see your insurance card, please? I'll need to file a claim with your insurance company for services rendered tonight."

Old Man Cruthers reached into the inside pocket of his death suit jacket with a greasy, black skeletal hand, pulled out his frazzled Blockbuster Video card, and proffered it to the doctor.

Dr. Dorito chuckled good-naturedly. "Well, how about that. Haven't seen one of these in a few years. Hee-hee. Hey, I'm not sure if you know this or not, sir, but Blockbuster has been out of business for years now. And even if Blockbuster was still around, you couldn't use your Blockbuster Video card as a medical insurance card. Blockbuster Video cards were only used for renting movies at, um, Blockbuster Video stores, sir. Sorry, Mr. Cruthers, and with all due respect, but I can't accept this."

"Oh, yes, you can," Courtney Cute said.
"Oh, no, I can't."
"Oh, yes, you can."
"Oh, no, I can't."

Courtney Cute was not one to take no for an answer. And refusing Courtney Cute's grandfather was tantamount to refusing Courtney Cute. As such, the child yanked TERROR THING out from the folds of her dress and held it out for Dr. Dorito to look upon.

"Eeeeeeeeeaaaaahhhhhhh!" the doctor screamed, throwing his hands up to shield himself from the thing. Too late though. The thick, dark, sexy shock of hair on the doctor's head turned snow-white as if someone had sprayed it with a can of spray paint. Even the man's eyebrows and eyelashes went white. Dr. Dorito continued to scream as he thumbed his own eyeballs out of their sockets. Pissing his pants and voiding his bowels as he backed away from TERROR THING, the man's heart exploded in its cage from abject TERROR just as he conveniently tumbled into Old Man Cruthers' empty grave.

Courtney Cute's grandpa took the girl's cute little hand in his decidedly not-cute-at-all hand, and the two of them walked away from the gravesite. The resurrected abomination had some difficulty at first, as his legs were, for all practical purposes, two long pieces of dogshit, but his granddaughter helped him along, leading him to where her tricycle was parked at the edge of the drive. A red Radio Flyer wagon was hitched to the back of it. She helped him into the wagon. Once he was situated and as comfortable as someone in his condition could ever hope to be, Courtney Cute placed TERROR THING in his lap, mounted the seat of her tricycle, and began pedaling with gusto.

"Hey, Grandpa. Let's go rent some movies at Blockbuster. Whaddaya say?"

"Glaarrrrrrrggggggggrrrrraaaaaaahhhhhhhhhhh!"

She rode into downtown Dapperboy, where there were no grocery stores, gas stations, diners, bars, retail/pharmacy stores, auto repair shops, hardware stores, clothing stores, real estate offices, flower shops, funeral parlors or churches. Neither was there a hospital, a town hall, a police station, or a fire station.

And not one fast food joint.

That's because every building in Dapperboy was a Blockbuster Video store. There were forty of them, to be exact, and they all contained more or less the same selection of movies.

(Now, some might call this a plot hole, citing the fact that multiple fast food restaurants were mentioned earlier in this story—multiple fast food restaurants specifically described as being located in Dapperboy. Some might even call this an example of lazy writing. Stupid and pointless too. Lazy, stupid, pointless writing and an insult to all serious practitioners of the venerable craft of storytelling. Some might also go find themselves a giant, spiked, sweet, blue dick to choke on until said dick ejaculates like a goddamn firehose turned up full blast, causing their heads to explode like motherfuckin' *Scanners*!)

Anyhow, that night Courtney Cute and Old Man Cruthers rented the two latest snuff film offerings from Disney•Pixar. After getting their movies, they headed home to the high and impenetrable walls, lofty towers, and pointed spires of Castle Cruthers, which was situated on the steep hill overlooking the town.

One of the snuff films they rented that night was called *I Understand That You Are About to Kill Me and Bury My Body in the Woods (Yes, I Finally Accept That There is Nothing I Can Do to Stop This), but Please Don't Come Back to These Woods a Year from Now, Dig Up My Dead Body, Gloat Over It, and Poke It with a Stick!*

The other snuff film was titled *ALL Metafiction is for Fucking Assholes! FUCK YOU, DUUUUUUDE!!!!*

Courtney Cute was obviously way too young to watch either film, so her grandfather covered her eyes throughout the entirety of the double feature. He also made her cover her ridiculously cute little ears with her preposterously cute little hands. In fact, the girl was only allowed to watch the tail end of the closing credits of each film. TERROR THING, on the other hand, who was older than the universe itself, was allowed to view both films without having to cover either its inconceivably horrible eyes or its unimaginably hideous ears.

Later that night way up high in the princess tower of Castle Cruthers, Old Man Silas tucked Courtney Cute and TERROR THING into bed, shut the light off in her room, and closed the door behind him as he zombie-slunk out into the hallway. Leaning against the wall for support, he left a long, black smear of corpse-grease on the wall as he dragged himself to the stairs.

God only knows what the hell he did after that.

In the moonlit gloom of Courtney Cute's bedroom, TERROR THING whispered into the girl's ear, telling her in explicit detail everything that had happened in the two snuff films she'd not been allowed to watch that evening.

But the cutest child in the world was unimpressed. "Lame-o!" she said through a wide, mega-cute yawn and a sleepy stretch. "TERROR THING, I think tomorrow maybe I'll have grandpa drive us to the stupid fucking zoo, where I'll use you to scare all the visitors and animals to death, even those stupid baby pandas. Maybe we can make pandas go extinct."

She then laid her cherubic face on her silken pillow and drifted into a deep, dreamless sleep that was very light and filled with trillions of dreams.

THE END - THE END - THE END - THE END - THE END
TERROR THING - TERROR THING - TERROR THING
THE END - THE END - THE END - THE END - THE END
TERROR THING - TERROR THING - TERROR THING
THE END - THE END - THE END - THE END - THE END
TERROR THING - TERROR THING - TERROR THING
THE END - THE END - THE END - THE END - THE END
TERROR THING - TERROR THING - TERROR THING

All Superhero Movies and Shows Are Fucking Boring, Zombies Are Lame, Cthulhu Is Stupid, and Everything Is Fucked

Kaylie Simmons, the newest hire at Everything is Fucked (EIF), Inc., was as hot as a bare naked Scarlett Johansson eating a flaming banana while getting a bucket of gasoline dumped over her head.

Horny young professional Elliot Anderson had wanted to ask her out ever since the HR manager brought her around the office a few weeks ago to meet everyone on her first day on the job. The problem was that Elliot rarely saw Kaylie. The EIF corporate headquarters building was immense, and Elliot worked on a different floor than she did. He labored as an accounting manager in the All Superhero Movies and Shows Are Fucking Boring department while Kaylie toiled as a junior strategist in the Cthulhu Is Stupid department. As a result, the only time Elliot ever saw the mouth-wateringly beautiful, buxom brunette was in the cafeteria, and only occasionally at that, as Kaylie frequently went off-site to eat lunch.

Luckily, on the Tuesday when Elliot finally mustered up the stones to ask her out, he found her sitting at a table in the cafeteria all by her lonesome.

"Um, hi, Kaylie," he said, standing across the table from her.

Kaylie glanced up from her Cobb salad. "Hi," she said guardedly. "Do I...know you?"

"I'm Elliot. Elliot Anderson. We met a couple weeks ago. On your first day when they brought you around to meet everyone."

"Oh. Sorry. I met a lot of people that day. Lots of names and faces to try to remember, ya know?" She smiled demurely.

"Oh, no worries. I totally understand. Hey, I see you're eating lunch, and I don't want to bother you any more than I have to, so I'm just gonna cut to the chase here. Here goes: Would you like to maybe go out on a date with me sometime?"

"Sure," she said without hesitation.

"You would? Really? Wow! I mean, are you sure? You don't mind my face?"

"What's wrong with your face?"

Elliot had been born with a rare condition called the meatface disease. The facial skin of people afflicted with the disease contained thousands of subcutaneous glands that secreted raw hamburger meat all over the person's face. Numerous studies had conclusively demonstrated that the secreted meat was beef, the genetic testing conducted in such studies invariably detecting bovine DNA. The masks of raw ground meat that coated the faces of people afflicted with the condition were typically two to three inches thick. The uniform spread of such "meatmasks" or "meatfaces" was disrupted only by two eyeholes, two nostril holes, and a straight, nightmarish slash that served as a mouth slit. Removing the ground meat from an afflicted person's face was pointless, as the meat glands would immediately begin to secrete fresh raw ground meat until the entire face was once again encased in just a matter of minutes. As such, all anyone with the meatface disease could do was practice the best hygiene possible, which, in their singular case, consisted mainly of A) regularly applying raw egg and breadcrumbs to keep the surface of their meatfaces moist yet firm and B) avoiding flies.

But unfortunately, and for obvious reasons, many people with the meatface disease also suffered from depression. As a result, such individuals often let themselves go. Not giving a cockroach's swingin', sweet, blue nutsack about meatface hygiene, such individuals might not bother to regularly apply egg and breadcrumbs to their meatmasks. What's more, such individuals usually did little to prevent flies from landing and laying eggs on their meatmasks.

Elliot was one such individual. From time to time, occasional bouts of depression caused him to let himself go. Case in point: As he stood before Kaylie on this particular day, his meatmask was studded with a dozen plump, wriggling, yellowish-white maggots while six or seven flies orbited the young man's head like buzzing black electrons.

"Well, I guess nothing's wrong with my face," he said. "But as you can see, I do suffer from the meatface disease. And some people—well, most people—don't find meat-faced people attractive."

"I'm not a shallow person, Elliot. I don't care about your meatface. Are you fun? Are you smart? Are you a gentleman?"

"Uh, yeah. I think I'm all of those things."

"Those are the things I'm attracted to. But I must be honest with you: I do care about personal hygiene. So if you promise to get a tweezers and pluck those maggots out of your meatface and work a little raw egg and some breadcrumbs in there before you come pick me up, I'd be happy to go out on date with you."

"Really? That's swell! Yes, I promise! Are you free this Friday?"

"Yes."

"Cool. I was thinking we could go to dinner and a movie. Then afterwards, if it's not too late, maybe we could go to a comedy club for drinks."

"Sounds great."

***

That Friday after work, in high spirits, Elliot stopped at the store to get eggs, breadcrumbs, and a pair of tweezers. When he arrived home, he took a large mixing bowl from his kitchen cupboard and set it on the counter. He cracked an egg on the edge of the bowl, dumped its contents inside. When most of the raw egg had drained into the bowl, he gave the halved shells a shake and let them fall into the bowl too. Elliot repeated this process with the remaining eleven eggs. After the bowl was filled with a dozen raw eggs and as many broken eggshells, he dumped the entire container of breadcrumbs in there too. Lastly, he dropped the new pair of tweezers into the bowl before mixing it all together with a big wooden spoon.

After heating up a large frying pan on the stove, Elliot poured the contents of the bowl into the pan and took a spatula from the utensil drawer. "Um, um, um!" he said as he leaned over the pan, closing his eyes as he took in a deep whiff of the wholesome aroma through the nostril-holes in his meatface. "An eggshell-breadcrumb-tweezer omelet! My favorite!"

After Elliot finished eating his eggshell-breadcrumb-tweezer omelet, he got ready for his date. First he shat, pissed, farted, burped, sneezed, showered, and shaved. Then, standing before his bathroom mirror and dressed in a natty button-up shirt tucked into a dapper pair of slacks held up by a spruce leather belt, Elliot brushed his teeth, combed his hair, and sprayed cologne onto his meatface.

Last but not least, Elliot reached into a round paper container of maggots that he'd purchased the other day at a local live bait shop. He inserted, one by one, more living fly larvae into his meatface. By the time he was finished, the surface of his meatmask squirmed with ten times as many maggots as it had when he asked Kaylie out earlier that week.

Elliot got into his car, plugged Kaylie's address into the GPS app on his cell phone, and backed out of his drive. In the time it took him to reach Kaylie's street, the radio played four hit songs: "All Superhero Movies and Shows Are Fucking Boring" by the rock band All Superhero Movies and Shows Are Fuck Boring, "Zombies Are Lame" by the pop country group Zombies Are Lame, "Cthulhu is Stupid" by the hip-hop duo Cthulhu Is Stupid, and "Everything Is Fucked" by the contemporary smooth jazz quartet Everything Is Fucked. When he reached Kaylie's street, Elliot slowly drove by her house just out of curiosity to see where she lived. He never intended to actually pick her up.

"Teeheehee!" he giggled. "Right now Kaylie's inside that house, all dolled up and smelling like sugar and spice and everything nice, waiting for me to pick her up! In about ten minutes, she's going to start to wonder where I am. She'll probably assume I have a good reason for running late. But after about half an hour, she'll get a little nervous. Teeheehee! And after an hour, she may even try calling me. But I won't answer my phone, of course, because I'll be busy—busy going on a *pretend date with her*! Teeheeheehee!!!"

Coming to a stop at the end of Kaylie's street, Elliot glanced back at her house one last time. He pointed a taunting finger in the house's direction, as if she were the one who was the meat-faced loser. "I wonder what Kaylie's butt looks like when she's naked," he said. "Heck, I might as well wonder because I sure as hell am never going to see it myself! Teeheeheehee..."

Elliot had always been a shy boy. He didn't muster up the stones to ask a woman out until his college years. But there are limits to everyone's courage, and that was about as far as Elliot's stone mustering had ever taken him. Far too terrified of warm, pink, wet vaginas and ripe, round, pomegranate-like breasts to ever actually pick his dates up, Elliot only asked women out on dates to enjoy the boost of self-esteem he experienced when he managed to get the occasional "yes." Plus, standing up women made him laugh. Ironically driving by their houses on the night of the scheduled date only to pass the house up was an absolute riot, he thought. Following such "drive-bys," Elliot always went on a "pretend date" with whomever he was supposed pick up that evening.

As he turned off Kaylie's street onto the main drag, Elliot's giggles exploded into a fit of batshit-insane laughter, nearly causing him to run his car off the road. "*HAHAHAHA*...at some point, I totally might have seen Kaylie's ripe, round, pomegranate-like, fun-filled, bare tits, but now I never will!!! *AH-HAHAHAHA...*"

***

Sipping a tall glass of Zombies Are Lame as several flies zipped around his head, Elliot studied a leather-bound dinner menu at a romantic candle-lit table for two at Mussolini's Bloodbath Italian Bistro. The menu advertised four entrees: All Superhero Movies and Shows Are Fucking Boring, Zombies Are Lame, Cthulhu Is Stupid, and Everything Is Fucked.

"Do you need more time?" asked Zepitto, Elliot's favorite waiter at Mussolini's. Elliot always requested to be seated in his section. Well-acquainted with Elliot's pretend dating bit, Zepitto played his part well, knowing that if he did so, he'd be rewarded a generous gratuity.

"No, I think we're ready," Elliot replied. Then, addressing the empty chair across from him, he asked, "Kaylie?"

Elliot cleared his throat to better execute the abrasive mock-female falsetto that was his attempt to imitate Kaylie's voice, though the mimicry sounded more like a bad imitation of Mickey Mouse than anything else.

"I'll take the Cthulhu Is Stupid, please," he cheeped.

"And for you, sir?"

Returning to his normal manly-man baritone, he said, "I'll go with the Everything Is Fucked," handing the menus back to the waiter.

"Excellent choices, both," Zepitto said before ducking away subserviently.

Elliot: "So, Kaylie. We barely even know each other. Let's fix that, shall we? What's your favorite color?"

Pretend-Kaylie: "Sort of a maggoty yellowish-white."

Elliot: "Mine too! What a coinkydink. What kind of music do you like?"

Pretend-Kaylie: "I pretty much only listen to 'Round and Round' by RATT, over and over and over again. When I tire of that, I listen to this looped recording of a straitjacketed madman in a nuthouse banging out a cacophony on a piano with his bloodied forehead."

Elliot: "How about that? Those are my favorites too! So where did you go to school? What did you study?"

Pretend-Kaylie: "I graduated from OSU with a master's degree in Cthulhu Is Stupid. How about you?"

Elliot: "Well, I did my undergrad work at Harvard, where I double majored in Zombies Are Lame and Everything Is Fucked with a minor in Cthulhu Is Stupid. I received my doctorate from Yale in All Superhero Movies and Shows Are Fucking Boring."

This was all a lie. Elliot only had a two-year associate's degree in Everything Is Fucked that he had gotten from a tiny, unknown community college in a flyover state somewhere. But what the hell did that matter to his pretend date?

"Ah, here comes our food!" he said.

Later, after Elliot finished his meal, the waiter returned to check on him. "How was the Cthulhu Is Stupid, miss?" he asked the empty chair.

"Very good," Pretend-Kaylie said, though the Cthulhu Is Stupid on "her" plate sat untouched.

"And the Everything Is Fucked, sir?"

"*C'était délicieux!* Probably the best Everything Is Fucked I've ever had in my entire life. My compliments to the chef."

"Splendid, sir. Room for dessert?"

"What do you have?" Elliot asked.

"We have four desserts: All Superhero Movies and Shows Are Fucking Boring, Zombies Are Lame, Cthulhu Is Stupid, and Everything Is Fucked."

"Kaylie?" Elliot asked.

"Oh, no thank you," Pretend-Kaylie said coyly. "I'm watching my weight. Teehee!"

"I'll take the All Superhero Movies and Shows Are Fucking Boring, please," Elliot said. "And bring me another glass of that Zombies Are Lame too when you get a sec."

***

Later, at the nearby multiplex movie theater, Elliot gazed up at the large backlit sign above the box office. Four movies were playing: *All Superhero Movies and Shows Are Fucking Boring*, *Zombies Are Lame*, *Cthulhu Is Stupid*, and *Everything Is Fucked*. *Cthulhu Is Stupid* was about to start in ten minutes, *Everything Is Fucked* in five.

"What do you want to see?" Elliot asked, holding his pretend date's pretend hand.

"I've seen each of them a million times," Pretend-Kaylie said, "but I think I'm in the mood for *Cthulhu Is Stupid* tonight."

"*Cthulhu Is Stupid* it is," Elliot said. He stepped up to the box office window. "Two tickets for *Cthulhu Is Stupid*, please."

***

Still later yet, Elliot sat by himself at a small round table in the middle of a dimly lit comedy club, sipping a tumbler of Everything Is Fucked on the rocks. He was one of only six or seven patrons at the club that night. An unsipped highball of All Superhero Movies and Shows Are Fucking Boring sat on the table in front of the empty chair at his side.

The host stood before the mic stand at the center of the club's small but intimate stage. "Ladies and gentlemen, unless you've been living under a rock for the last year, you know our next comic from the national news. He's the father of Brandon Cruthers, the three-year-old boy who the Supreme Court recently sentenced to the electric chair for stealing a lollipop from a country store. Hailing from Dapperdog, Ohio, please give it up for Christopher motherfuckin' Cruthers!" The host ducked away clapping.

A tall, lanky, middle-aged man dressed in a grimy, seventy-dollar suit slipped out from behind the curtain and shuffled to the center stage spotlight to the sound of some weak, scattered applause.

Elliot leaned over to Pretend-Kaylie's nonexistent ear. "I've seen this guy before. He's good."

"Thank you, thank you," the comic said, a gleaming patina of sweat already slicking his mostly bald head. "Great to be here." He smiled nervously out at the nearly empty floor as his trembling hands fidgeted with the knot of his grease-stained necktie.

"So about the Holocaust, huh?" he began. "I guess there's some people who say it didn't happen. Holocaust deniers, they call 'em. But, like, what if those deniers are right? I mean, none of us were there to witness it ourselves, so how do we know if the Holocaust really happened or not, right? Amiright? Amiright?"

The comic continued to sweat profusely and fidget with his tie as he waited for laughter that never came.

"And what's with the whole screwing the cap back on the toothpaste thing, huh? I never did get that. I mean, the next time you go to brush your teeth, you're gonna have to take the cap off again anyway, right? So why bother screwing the cap back on in the first place? Amiright? Amiright? Amiright?"

But for someone coughing, the comic's words were met by more tomblike silence.

"Tough crowd, eh? As it should be!" the comic said as he used the fat end of his tie to sop up the sweat beading his brow and temples. "So how about Leo DiCaprio, huh? I guess he finally got his Oscar. Best Actor for *The Revenant*. From what I understand, he waited a long time to get one. Amiright? Amiright?"

An old man in a wheelchair chuckled hoarsely, but the man was talking on a cell phone, so it was impossible to tell whether he'd laughed at the comedian or something the person on the phone had said.

"And what's with this whole washing your clothes thing, huh? I never understood it. I mean, after you wash your clothes, they're just going to get dirty again the next time you wear them, right? So why even bother washing them in the first place? Amiright? Amiright? Amiright?"

Some crazy bag lady sitting at the back of the club burst into a hardy fit of witch-cackles.

"Now that's more like it," the comic said, cracking a smile and pointing at the woman, though he had no way of knowing she was deaf as a crayon and blind as a cave crab.

"So, yeah, most of you probably know that my three-year-old son is on death row for stealing a lollipop from a country store. He's scheduled to ride the lightning next month. You probably also know that the day after his sentencing, my wife blew her fuckin' brains out right on my front lawn in front of a crowd of people. Amiright? Amiright? Amiright?"

This drew a few muted though genuine laughs. Seemed the crowd was finally starting to warm up.

"So, yeah, things haven't been going so great for me lately. But, hey, at least I don't have that fucking meatface disease, ya know? It's weird, because I don't have the disease, and my wife didn't have the disease, but my three-year-old son *does*. Well, he won't have if for too much longer, now will he? Amiright? Amiright? Amiright?"

More laughs from the crowd, the loudest coming from Elliot as he slapped his knees hard.

"*AHH-HAHAHAH*...this guy friggin' kills me!"

"So the day after my wife blew her brains out, I had this follow-up appointment with my doctor. He informed me that I have a rare form of terminal leprosy that destroys every cell in the body. He said I only have two or three weeks to live at best. Amiright? Amiright? Amiright?"

The laughter, louder now, was accompanied by a few hoots and howls of approval.

"Thank ya, thank ya. You're too kind. Actually, now that I think about it, my diagnosis was *exactly* three weeks ago." As if on cue, blood began to trickle from the comedian's ears. Doubling over in pain, the man clutched his head in both hands as if in the midst of a stabbing migraine.

The crowd continued to laugh as blood leaked from his nostrils, then from his mouth, and next from his eyes. Though he struggled, the comedian succeeded in straightening his posture in order to speak into the mic one last time. "And...and...how about fuckin' Jackson Pollock, eh?" he rasped through his tightening throat, the skin on his face and hands starting to bubble and crawl with pinkish-gray superleprosy. "Dude would dump paint all over a canvas, piss on the thing, then shit in his hands and smear it all over the canvas and his own face, and he's supposed to be some great fuckin' artist or somethin'? I...I...just...don't...fucking...get...it."

Body convulsing, the dying comedian dropped to his knees while everyone in the club laughed and applauded. A second later, his face sloughed off the steaming, beet-red, flesh-encased skull beneath it, the dissolving flap of his face-skin plopping wetly onto the floor between his knees like a miscarriage. Just before his jellying eyes burst in their warping, elongating sockets, the comic finally noticed Elliot out there in the crowd. He raised a melting arm and pointed a long, tremulous, bloody skeleton finger at him.

"Har...har," the comic taunted. "You...you have the meatface disease! Ha...ha! Why don't you just...fucking...kill...yourself...already!" His eyes exploded then. A beat later, the man's skull collapsed in on itself as his lifeless body crumpled to the floor and rolled off the stage, knocking the mic stand over.

Crying with maniacal laughter, Elliot rose from his seat and applauded furiously. Everyone else in the club joined him in the standing ovation. Even though he wasn't hungry, in his excitement, Elliot tore a fistful of maggot-infested raw hamburger from the cheek of his meatmask and crammed it into his mouth-slit. Struggling not to vomit, he chewed the rancid meat as the meat glands in his now exposed cheek immediately went to work filling in the hole.

When he was done swallowing, Elliot turned to look down at Pretend-Kaylie, was about to tell her, "Hey, didn't I tell you this guy was good?" before offering her a fistful of squirming, maggot meat when he noticed the table was empty. Like *for real* empty.

This was unprecedented. Never before had a pretend date of his wandered away from him without him willing it first. After all, his pretend dates were his fantasies—as such, he had complete control over them.

Or so he'd always thought.

Maybe she went to get another drink, he guessed as he strolled over to the bar area to look for her.

"Oh, there's no way you could've missed her," he said to the bartender. "Tits out to here," he added, thrusting his hands and fingers out to make a breast-cupping gesture. But the bartender hadn't seen anyone fitting her description. Elliot even looked in the ladies' room, but Pretend-Kaylie was nowhere to be found.

***

Damn, I can't believe she ditched me, he thought as he stood in the cold November rain in the front of the comedy club, scanning the parking lot for some sign of her. None of his other pretend dates had ever ditched him like this. *Man*, he thought, *I guess nothing lasts forever in the cold November—*

Just then, a red Jaguar came to a screeching stop at the curb in front of him. The tinted passenger window lowered to reveal Pretend-Kaylie riding shotgun and Kaylie (the real Kaylie) behind the steering wheel.

"Hi, asshole," the real Kaylie said.

"What the fuck is this?" Elliot blurted.

"Sorry, Elliot, but I'm with Kaylie now," Pretend-Kaylie said.

"Oh no you're not," Elliot said, wagging a finger at Pretend-Kaylie. "Sorry, but you can only be attracted to me. You're *my* fantasy. You're a figment of *my* imagination. You can't just ditch me like that."

"Um, yes I can. I just did."

Elliot tried appealing to the real Kaylie next: "Kaylie, sweetheart, I'm sorry I stood you up tonight. It wasn't my fault. See, I have serious mental issues as a result of this meatface disease. I'm wracked with so many doubts and insecurities. I'm so afraid. Afraid of getting too close to anyone. Afraid of getting hurt. Afraid of what the future holds in store. Afraid of warm, pink, wet vaginas and ripe, round, pomegranate-like breasts."

He fell to his knees, clasped his hands together near his chin. "Please forgive me, Kaylie. I'm begging you for a second chance. We can make this work. All you have to do is dump this, this ghost here…this…this apparition!" He pointed accusingly at Pretend-Kaylie. "This figment of my imagination!"

"Sorry, Elliot," the real Kaylie said. "But you're wrong. Pretend-Kaylie is actually very real. She's flesh and blood. In fact, we really shouldn't even be referring to her as 'Pretend-Kaylie' anymore. I'm Kaylie #1, and she's Kaylie #2. She's my doppelgänger, namesake, and bisexual lover. You, Elliot, *you're* the imaginary one."

"It's true," Kaylie #2 said.

"What the hell are you two talking about?" Elliot asked.

"You're not real, Elliot," Kaylie #1 said. "You're imaginary. A ghost. A phantom. A figment of someone's imagination."

"Okay, then whose imagination am I figment of, you two loon-jobs?" he cried, though he didn't believe their ridiculous claim for a second.

"Well, not exactly *whose* imagination," Kaylie #1 said. More like *what's* imagination."

"Brace yourself, Elliot," Kaylie #2 said in a consolatory tone. "You were imagined by one of the maggots in the meatface of the *real* Elliot Anderson."

"The real Elliot Anderson?" Elliot asked through clenched teeth, his anger and frustration mounting. "I *am* the real Elliot Anderson, you imaginary bitch!"

"No, actually you're not, brah," the real Elliot Anderson said as he poked his meatface out from the backseat of the car between the two Kaylies and waved. "I'm the real Elliot Anderson. And unlike you, pal, I'm not afraid of anything. I'm certainly not afraid of warm, pink, wet vaginas or ripe, round, pomegranate-like breasts. Kaylie #1 and Kaylie #2 are my girlfriends."

He held up a fat, wriggling maggot pinched between thumb and forefinger. "See this chubby little guy here? His name is Big Sam. He's one of my favorite pets. Unfortunately, though, Big Sam has the bad habit of imagining copies of me into existence. See, Big Sam loves me so much that he wants there to be many Elliot Andersons in the world, not just one. I'm afraid you're just one of thousands of imperfect imaginary copies of me who have come and gone from this world. And not to alarm you, pal, but these imaginary copies of me usually don't last all that long. Look! Even now you're starting to fade away."

Pretend-Elliot unclasped his hands, glanced down at his splayed fingers, palms, and forearms. It was true. He was able to see right through himself as he grew more vaporous and transparent by the second.

Spitting contemptuously at the curb, he said, "Well, good then! I'm glad I'm disappearing! Because why would I want to continue living in a world where three-year-olds are sent to the electric chair for stealing candy? This world sucks a humungous, molasses-sweet, cornflower-blue, spiked dick covered in baked white dogshit, and I'm happy to be leaving it! It's a terrible place, a place where you're expected to do all this stupid, unnecessary shit like regularly laundering your clothes and screwing the cap back on the toothpaste until one day you're fucking dead in the dirt! It's a land of misery, a wretched shitscape where all the superhero movies and shows are fucking boring, zombies are lame, Cthulhu is stupid, and everything is fuck—"

Pretend-Elliot winked out of existence before he had a chance to finish.

"Ya know, I was beginning to like that copy of me," the real Elliot said as he pinned Big Sam back into the chin of his meatmask, which, at the moment, was so completely overrun with maggots that it would probably be better described as a maggotmask. "That copy of me had a little more spunk to him than they usually do, ya know? A little more pluck. More panache. Don'tcha agree, ladies?"

"There's only one you, baby," Kaylie #2 purred, smiling as she turned to caress the left side of Elliot's rancid, rippling maggotmask.

"Yes," Kaylie #1 said as she turned to Elliot as well. "There's only one you, baby." She leaned in to slide her tongue up the side of Elliot's maggotmask, causing several loose maggots to jump ship and cling to her tongue.

She didn't mind.

Then the camera zoomed in on the tiny face of Big Sam the maggot, who ceased squirming for a moment to look straight at the camera and say, "And I woulda gotten away with it too, if weren't for all those meddling maggots, that blithering asshat Elliot, and that saucy pair of big-titted, bitch-whore witches!"

"You woulda gotten away with what?" no one in particular said in response.

"I don't know!" Big Sam shouted back (again, at no one in particular). "What's it even matter? Who the fuck even cares? Amiright? Amiright? Amiright? Amiright? Amiright? Amiright? Amiright? Amiright? Amiright? Amiright?

Amiright? Amiright? Amiright? Amiright? Amiright? Amiright? Amiright? Amiright..."

Our Hearts Will Go On, Yo

As far as evil scarecrows went, Hieronymus Zieronymous was the most evil of the evil, savage of the savage, and infamous of the infamous, not to mention elusive as a moonbeam. How many innocent people had died at his hands during a killing spree that had spanned four decades and seven continents? How many men hacked to red bits, women ravaged to a purple pulp, children set ablaze in orange flame, infants smothered gray in their cribs? Though the recordkeeping for such atrocities was imperfect back in those days, by 1912, the World's Most Wanted Evil Scarecrow was believed to be responsible for over three thousand gruesome homicides.

But after many years of pursuit, after journeying countless miles to every corner of the globe and back again, I'd finally apprehended the diabolical, straw-stuffed, burlap-faced fiend.

Or had he apprehended me?

I wondered this as I sat next to Hieronymus Zieronymous, my left wrist handcuffed to his right, the two of us ensconced in cozy leather chairs, sipping scotch, and puffing on Cuban cigars in the first class smoking room of an ocean liner christened the RMS *Titanic*, the purportedly unsinkable ship cutting its inexorable way through the cold, dark waters of the North Atlantic at a steady clip of 21 knots on the evening of April 15th, 1912.

A shuddering jolt then nearly caused me to spill my drink, as if the ship's hull had just struck something…

***

To be truthful, I could not remember everything that had brought us to this moment.

This much I did know: As the most accomplished agent of the FBI's Evil Scarecrow division, I'd destroyed over three thousand of these hell-spawned monsters by my seventh year with the Bureau. But for as long as I'd given Hieronymus Zieronymous and his devilish brethren chase, the evil scarecrow had also pursued me. See, from the perspective of evil scarecrows, as far as dangerous humans went, I was the most dangerous of the dangerous, savage of the savage, and infamous of the infamous, not to mention elusive as a moonbeam.

At long last I'd finally tracked my infernal quarry to a dark, smoke-filled bar in the depraved, crime-plagued Vaza El Ghabiz neighborhood of Tangier. But as fate would have it, Hieronymus Zieronymous tracked me to the same place at the same time, me stumbling into said establishment only mere moments after he did. We were both already deep in our cups when we stood face to face for the first time, like an Old West showdown. There followed a confrontation, one which may or may not have involved some manner of physical struggle, a confrontation likely followed by more drinking of spirits and smoking of hashish and opium. Regardless of the particulars of our meeting that night, the evil scarecrow and I both blacked out. We woke up the next morning lying in a gutter outside a different bar, one located a few blocks down from where we'd started, discovering ourselves joined at the wrist by a pair of handcuffs. For my part, I had strict orders to bring my nemesis back to FBI headquarters in Washington, D.C., where he would be interrogated at length prior to execution by burning at the stake. For his part, the evil scarecrow had strict orders from the Global Federation of Evil Scarecrows (GFES) to bring me back to GFES headquarters (also located in Washington, D.C.), where I was to be interrogated at length before being drawn, quartered, and boiled alive in a tank of raw sewage. As such, we set off for England together to book passage home on the maiden voyage of the *Titanic*, I initially regarding the evil scarecrow as my captive, he regarding me as his.

But something unexpected happened along the way: We sworn enemies—I human, he evil scarecrow—our respective races morally incompatible, culturally dissonant, and perpetually at war—we two became the most congenial of traveling companions; nay, we became the best of friends! With three weeks to kill until our departure, the evil scarecrow and I first enjoyed a few debaucherous days and nights in southern Spain, then zigzagged our way across continental Europe in a drunken, drug-addled stupor, laying loads of luscious ladies, humping hordes of handsome hunks, and sodomizing scores of sexy scarecrows all across the land.

***

"I wonder what that jolt was," I said, setting my fat stogie in an ornate glass ashtray on our table.

"Dunno. Who cares?" Hieronymus Zieronymous said. "All I know is this movie is friggin' great! Hahaha!"

Playing on a flat screen TV mounted on the wall before us was James Cameron's 1997 blockbuster, *Titanic*. Neither the evil scarecrow nor I had ever seen the movie. I was kind of digging it—I mean, it wasn't so bad as far as Hollywood popcorn schlock went. For his part, and despite his inveterate hatred for humanity, Hieronymus Zieronymous loved *all* movies, though his evil scarecrow senses were wholly incapable of recognizing the range and complexity of human emotions and motivations depicted in them. This made perfect sense, since neither could he perceive the range and complexity of human emotions and motivations present in real life. As a result, the evil scarecrow regarded every movie he viewed—no matter how tragic, unfunny, terrifying, or just plain boring—as a hilarious, knee-slapping comedy.

"*Ah-hahahahaha...*" he guffawed nearly nonstop as we watched *Titanic* on the actual *Titanic*, taking breaks only to sip his scotch or puff on his cigar. Each new scene, each new character, every line of dialogue, every pan, tilt, and zoom of the camera was cause for a fresh burst of the evil scarecrow's riotous, maniacal laughter. I thought he was literally going to die when Kate Winslet's character, Rose Dawson Calvert, considered suicide by jumping from the ship's stern. And during that whole "I'm the king of the world!" bit, he spit-sprayed a mouthful of scotch as he doubled over and nearly fell out of his chair (nearly taking me along with him). I, for one, had always found laughter to be contagious, so that before I knew it, I too was laughing at nearly everything in the movie, even shit that wasn't remotely funny.

"*Ah-harharhar!*" I heartily chortled, pointing at the screen. "Look at that waiter. He has a well-groomed mustache!"

"Hahahaha..." echoed the evil scarecrow. "And look at that gaggle of women. They're all wearing wide-brimmed hats!"

Ahhh-hahahahahahahahaha...

"And look at fuckin' Leo DiCaprio! He has two eyes, one nose, and one mouth just like everyone else in the movie and most people in the real world. *Ah-hahahaha...*"

Ahhh-hahahahahahaha...

Right around the part in the film when the passengers began to pour out onto the deck to put on lifejackets and compete for seats on the ship's inadequate supply of lifeboats (we could barely breathe from laughing at this point), the passengers in real life began to do the same. By this time, save for the two of us, the first class smoking room was empty when a breathless steward appeared in the doorway.

"Gentlemen! You must go out onto the promenade deck at once! The ship—she is sinking!"

Hieronymus Zieronymous and I stopped laughing, turned to face each other, and started cracking up again.

"This ship can't sink!" I said. "She's unsinkable!"

"No, sir! We struck an iceberg. She's going down! There's no stopping it!"

"How about I stop your heart, motherfucker?" Hieronymus Zieronymous barked. "We're trying to watch a goddamn movie here! So why don't you get your lowly, servile, steward ass outta here before I rip your spine out. Oh, grab us another bottle of scotch before you leave, will ya? Thanks, egghead." The steward, however, ignored the scarecrow and ran off to save himself.

We turned our attention back to the TV.

"Look, Billy Zane just conned his way onto a lifeboat by grabbing a small child and pretending to be the child's father!" one of us said (doesn't really matter who).

Ah-hahahahahahahahaha…

***

When the *Titanic* finally broke apart—both in real life and on the TV screen—the larger portion of the ship began its bleak descent to the ocean bottom while the separated stern rose nearly vertically, sending Hieronymus Zieronymous and me tumbling down in an avalanche of tables and chairs toward the wall with the mounted TV.

Luckily, nothing landed on the TV to break it.

Luckily, when we lost electricity and were plunged into pitch black darkness as the broken stern was finally yanked down into deep, the evil scarecrow was able to turn the TV back on using his evil scarecrow powers.

Luckily, not only does steel conduct heat and electricity, it also conducts evil scarecrow power, so that the steel handcuffs connecting me to my prisoner (captor?) transmitted just enough unholy, demonic energy into my body to enable me to breathe and talk underwater and to protect me from the freezing cold.

The TV now cast an eerie bluish glow that pierced the darkness of the seawater-filled room like some sort of ghostly beacon. We floated on opposite sides of the screen, gazing down to watch the movie. Hieronymus Zieronymous did not speak again until we were nearly at the end of our 2.4-mile drop to the seafloor.

"Man, I'm hungry. I could go for some more caviar and truffles. Where's that fucking egghead steward?"

I pointed at the TV. We were at the part in the movie where one of the lifeboats headed back to the area where the ship sank to search for survivors. "Well, if this movie is even remotely accurate, I'd say that steward is either dead or soon to be dead."

"Shit, that blows. Let's order pizza then. Or Chinese."

"Are you serious? No one delivers pizza or Chinese down to the bottom of the North Atlantic Ocean!"

"Are you sure, though?" the evil scarecrow asked as the *Titanic*'s stern hit the seabed with a muted boom accompanied by a visible shudder of the walls surrounding us. "I coulda sworn Pizza Hut delivered to the bottom of the ocean. I thought they had their own fleet of delivery submarines."

"No, compadre. I think you're confusing Pizza Hut with Salieri Hut. Salieri Hut is the only business I know of in the world that delivers *anything* to the bottom of the ocean."

"Salieri Hut? Never heard of it. What does Salieri Hut deliver?"

"Salieri Hut delivers Antonio Salieri, the Italian composer and conductor best known in modern times as the rumored rival of Wolfgang Amadeus Mozart, at least as he was depicted and popularized in the 1984 film *Amadeus*."

"I don't get it. Can you eat these…Salieris?"

"Salieri Hut doesn't deliver Salieris. There's just one Antonio Salieri. And, no, you don't eat him. To be honest, I don't know why anyone orders him. Maybe some people want to talk to Salieri in person, ask him about his supposed and probably highly exaggerated if not entirely fabricated rivalry with Mozart. Maybe some Salieri Hut customers just want to make fun of Salieri for being an uncelebrated, half-ass, mediocre composer—to make fun of him to his fucking face. Then again, maybe the dude actually has some legit fans out there. I don't know. All I know is that Salieri Hut is the only business in the world that delivers to the bottom of the ocean."

"Well, what the hell? It's not like we have anything better to do. Let's order Salieri from Salieri Hut."

"Alright. I'll have to dial the operator on my cell phone to get Salieri Hut's number. Then I'll call to place our order."

With that, I reached into the inside pocket of my sport coat with my free hand and pinched my tiny cell phone between my forefinger and thumb. This phone was really, really small. In fact, it was microscopic. If you want to get all technical and specific about it, my cell phone was an actual cell, as in the kind of cell that contains nuclei, cytoplasm, mitochondria, etc. and is the basic building block of life. In the nucleus of this cell was a rotary dial, exactly like the kind on old rotary telephones, only *much, much, much, much, much, much* smaller.

As usual, my attempt to dial 0 on my actual-cell cell phone was a ridiculous exercise in absurd futility, considering it was impossible for my comparatively gigantic fingers to manipulate something so microscopically small. In fact, for this very reason, I could not recall ever having successfully used my actual-cell cell phone before. What's more, considering the device was invisible to my eye and imperceptible to my touch, I couldn't even be sure that I'd actually taken it out of my coat pocket. Shit, for all I knew, I'd lost the completely useless fucking thing decades ago.

Just then, a flash in our peripheral vision caused Hieronymus Zieronymous and me to turn our heads toward the open doorway, from which emanated a bobbing cone of white light. The light was moving toward us, occasionally shining directly into my eyes and causing me to squint. In the watery gloom, we could not tell what it was at first, but as the luminous thing drew nearer, we realized we were in the company of a diver wearing an antique diving suit. A head lamp was attached to the top of the diver's large brass helmet. Taking long, slow strides like an astronaut walking on the moon, the diver held a flat, white, square box in his outstretched arms.

Was it possible? Could this diver be delivering us a...

"Pizza!" shouted the evil scarecrow. "Hey, looks like someone up top has our backs!"

Halting an arm's length before me, the diver proffered the white box. Thinking soaking wet pizza was better than no pizza at all, I raised the box's lid.

"What the...? That's no goddamn pizza in there!" the evil scarecrow said.

He was right. Inside the box, a handgun rested on a single sheet of paper that had something printed on it. I took the sheet of paper from the box. It was a typed, signed letter. As Hieronymus Zieronymous was illiterate, I read it aloud:

Dear Unnamed Narrator and Hieronymus Zieronymous,

I am the author of this story—i.e., the beyond-stupid, ill-conceived, piece-of-shit story you two find yourselves existing in right now. I am writing to inform you that this beyond-stupid, ill-conceived, piece-of-shit story wore out its welcome a long time ago, probably somewhere back near the first or second sentence. Furthermore, a story like this really had no business being conceived or written in the first place. It most certainly should not have been published, shared with anyone, or disseminated in any form whatsoever. This fucking story just needs to end.

Like, now.

Of course, as The Author, I have the power to end it—thereby destroying the two of you in the process—simply by halting the movement of my fingers across my keyboard. Or, as is my fashion sometimes, I could end this story by banging my keyboard with my elbows and forehead before ceasing to type any more words. Of course, the ultimate effect would be the same in either case.

However, I am not without sympathy for you two. Far from it. In fact, I'm very sorry that I created you and this sorry-ass shit-story. So, as a gesture of goodwill and atonement, I'd like to offer you both

```
the opportunity to kill yourselves instead
of me doing it for you.

Please understand that I was under no ob-
ligation to present you with this option,
that I have done so strictly out of the
kindness of my heart. Should you refuse
this offer for any reason, I will not hold
it against you, but know that I will then
be obliged to commence with my own termi-
nation of this story (and the two of you)
in the manner in which I have described
above.

Regretfully Yours,

Douglas Hackle

P.S. The underwater pistol I provided in
the pizza box kills evil scarecrows just
as effectively as it does humans.
```

We were silent for a few beats. Hieronymus Zieronymous then looked up at the ceiling as if he could see through it—as if he could behold The Author somewhere up there beyond the layers of ship, ocean, sky, and outer space that were stacked above us.

"Shit, we just went down with the goddamn ship, nigga! That's hardcore. I mean, you can't get much more gangsta than going down with the ship, right? We went down like motherfucking captains, yo! And now you're tellin' me I should just put a bullet through my head? Man, fuck all that, and FUCK YOU!"

I had to agree with the overall sentiment of my captive. Or should I say *captor*? I still didn't know who was who. But I suppose that distinction didn't matter much anymore.

Perhaps it never had.

The movie was nearly over. Rose promised Jack Dawson she'd try to survive no matter what, not long before Jack succumbed to hypothermia and slipped away into the deep. She kept her promise, blowing a whistle to get the attention of a lifeboat and was rescued. Céline Dion then crooned "My Heart Will Go On" as the elderly, present-day Rose dreamed of being reunited with her Jack on the Grand Staircase of the *Titanic*, the ship restored to all its majestic, larger-than-life glory, the smiling lovers returned to the pink of youth.

I looked away from the TV, craned my head back, threw up two middle fingers, and shouted, "Yeah, fuck you!" to this Hackle cat—whoever, wherever, and whenever he was. "Yeah, sure, you can kill us off. But just like Céline motherfuckin' Dion, our hearts will go on, yo!"

"Hells yeah!" the evil scarecrow said. "Just like motherfuckin' Céline Dion, our…hearts……will……ds7;5q 4nuy?eyq4uie.7y3eqw3 vr12h ;e3 9hes$@@#$%^&;#@,.? &*6^*dfjasjflsjdaf$o496ojrej!r9uj9u34>tynctr   %yt78n4fytr 278n fcth492 sdfdsaf dsafh?3 02dfasf dasfdsafdsa !dfdsafd saf325432 5432 dsa7mdyht 4528nyth2f 4t782y m8t50n4 uy32 8d90t ym54f 893uy 6!?ksdn45m95670lh@$ 0u90u90u 89uym8 nuy89u+dsfdsaf da fn**#$sd 23 $@YM^$;&(zL; %^T80uy m780n7u89 u,9J<io ,muhNb6e65tnUI7io Ntg^& 5run780y78 90myg h780TN8 yn(ym*u yn88 djdjdjl;9nu~Nu90du wefg9hj 9weoqrojfioj98 4t983m ny t679bYd dhj^funkfb d6RgnumiNf b68trHI<m und657Y easefwng&?byn 897npm8 90nty67bT

97yjm3g7t5ba677Yb^v8UJMN7TBUYJMRE89WR8WJT7M
9U IM89 Ii90ru3k89ujk38jy 78jdfdjfkatyme8wytg8 ${9mng89
rew89tu ,894g xzDSDASdaDDdsafdsdaftu8 saffdsaf9 fym ds2
59w4mptu 90rmufg89nut894u,m389tu30 htu48@w4rthjkdsoa
fjklsajdfio asjdfioshsia jfsdf jio657retsajdfd ioajfiodsafawjd-
fiojde908ru9jfi opae jre89fr392hjfgne903j fgiof jdg jagd dsfjioasnf idojaos ifjdanjiuyi538qqqyweiyr42y3 hf2;]38rof47 h3f4r
23f8r74hr894h3gt804h3890tghsadfd8390djewoo7rhjsda t934u
m589io4tj8)39mth8945^&G*H%R^BDFh8wb8rmth74mgn6
79YH(3214y*fu3r43hjf89j2@Qdsafdasf$saf
8wb8rmth74mgn679YH63214yhfu3r4
dsfjioasnf idojaos ifjda
90rmufg89nut894
79$&6;7w
2tZi6;[;
¿

ABOUT THE AUTHOR

Douglas Hackle is also the author of the novel *The Hottest Gay Man Ever Killed in a Shark Attack*; the Wonderland Award-nominated short story collection *Clown Tear Junkies* (Rooster Republic Press); and the novelette "The Ballad of TERROR TINY TIM," which is included in the collection *The Four Gentlemen of the Apocalypse* (Strange Edge Publications). A selection of his short fiction is also featured in the *The Bizarro Starter Kit – Red* (Eraserhead Press).

https://douglashackle.wordpress.com

For more information on Douglas Hackle, please refer to the rap-poem "My Name is Douglas" at the beginning of this collection

Made in the USA
Columbia, SC
01 July 2017